My Trials and Errors

Reflections of a Single Father
James R. Simms

My Trials and Errors
Copyright © 2010 by James R. Simms
Published by James R Simms
Edited by Danielle Reed

ISBN 978-0-615-42046-2

Printed in USA

Table of Contents

Dedication

This book is dedicated to my family and friends for being there for me in my time of need. All the support mentally, financially and spiritually helped me cope and come out on top. Thank you Mom, Aunt Connie (Rest in Peace) and Ms. Tashia Echols.

Forward

James is the loving father of two precious gems. When his children were taken from him abruptly, I watched him struggle with demons to get them back. He had the devil on one shoulder telling him to get his kids back by force. On the other shoulder, I saw an angel telling him to do the right thing so that he wouldn't lose the kids forever.

For as long as I have known him, he has struggled to put his past behind him and start to live his life on the straight and narrow. He once told me, that in order to move ahead, he had to give up everything associated with his past. Once he was able to accomplish that, his physical struggle became great but as I saw it, his spiritual struggle became greater.

However, James is a man of solid faith, emotion, and spirit. He is a man of his word who truly values his family unit and those he holds dear to him. If ever I need someone in my corner he is and will always be there for me.

Thank you James for all you do, have done and will continue to do to lift those around you emotionally, spiritually and physically.

Tashia Echols

Introduction

Parenting is a hard job with two parties working together, so just imagine how hard it is when there is only one party working for the well-being and stability needed to raise children.

As parents, you have to understand that it is not about you, but the welfare of your kids. You have to commit to that with all your being.

Nowadays, we should consider it lucky to have two parents who care and at the least one who will sacrifice the world for us. I am that parent who was willing to go to the end of the world for my kids.

I am not alone.

There are plenty of parents out there that will do the same. My story is meant to empower them to do more and to be there for their kids, no matter what. It is my hope that my story will inspire all parents to do better. Mostly, this book is written for males who may have gone through similar situations—please remember that just because she says it does not make it law. You can be part of your kid's life.

I know that sometimes it is a great feat to deal with the other parent and the court system scares a lot of us. However, truth be told, the system is there to help everyone. Unfortunately, when it comes to fairness in court dealings between the sexes, it seems that the courts tend to lean one way and we as males have a lot to do with that notion too. If you looked at this situation statistically, you would see that the majority of men fit into that stereotype—i.e. not taking care of their kids, or just don't know where to start or feel that they have a chance.

I'm here to dispel all of those stereotypes. We do care and are interested. From one to another who did not know how…I started with love.

I loved my kids enough to find out what I had to do to be in their lives. I did research. The love for your kids should enable you to go above and beyond for them, but first you have to get rid of the fear. The fear of the unknown, fear that if you try, you will fail because you have the deck stacked against you because you're a man. Here is the inside scoop men—you have the same rights to your kids as women do. Equal rights.

I grew up hearing the horror stories about men and women and custody—how men were subjected to cruel tactics. Men leaving women alone to raise kids by themselves and child support were a man's kryptonite and a woman's tool to destroy him. Child support should not be a bad word; it's your responsibility as a parent to take care of your kids. So with all of that said, here is a road map for those to protect your kids and yourself.

And this is not for just in case. In fact I wish that all relationships could result in marriage and a happily ever after ending, but for the ones that don't, knowing that there is hope for you in regards to your rights to being in your kid's life, first and foremost is become informed. Each state has their own process for securing rights to your children. Start by stepping up to be recognized as a parent. Establish parental rights either by (if you were around when the child was born), signing the birth certificate, followed by a blood test. The blood test may seem a little bit too much, but watch enough television and you already know, there have been cases that the child or children were not the man's and after a bad breakup he still had to pay. Legally, without filing, the man has no rights to the child. So filing is very important.

Legitimating your kids is the next step. This will involve you going to your local courthouse clerk's office and requesting the paperwork. More than likely you will be required to take a class or seminar. Fill out a child support worksheet and if you are not sure how—just ask. What hurts you the most is when the system has to come after you for child support. Then they give no consideration for you, your financial situation nothing. When you voluntary sign up for child support, they work with you instead of against you. Speaking from experience, it's better this way. Following these steps will assure your place in your kid's life at some capacity.

Remember not all situations are going to be perfect, but your involvement in your kid's life will pay off. You all will reap the benefits. The other key to your success is persistence. This process will be an uphill battle—sorry but that's just the way it is and you are very capable of completing the task at hand.

In most cases you will need a lawyer to represent you in court. Help yourself and the lawyer out, do your homework, and most lawyers will not do their best for you if you do not show interest and passion. Prepare your case. Remember you are proving to the court system why you are entitled to be in your kid's life. Write a letter to the judge presiding over your case, not just one but plenty—I would suggest a letter a week. This will ensure that you are not just the stereotypical and statistical image they may have of you, and also shows that you care.

Unfortunately, men sometimes get the raw deal—especially if they do not show interest in the case, but showing interest makes a world of difference. This is a piece of the road map that I followed to get me where I am today. It took a lot of hard work, determination, patience and faith. Hopefully my story will inspire another person, help put things in perspective and be a learning tool.

Here is my story about a very important time in my life that changed me forever. Enjoy!

Humble Beginnings

It was early October, when she left. A note on the door in her handwriting telling me to pay the electric bill and that my daughter was over her girlfriend's house.

So far from the life I had envisioned for my family and now I had to try and put pieces back together and manage this twist of fate.

Before we met, I admit I lived a double life. I worked full time and sold drugs on the side to supplement my lifestyle. Needless to say, I was a very busy man and most of the women that I had come across were one night stands and jump-offs, nothing serious or long term.

Before I met her, I had experienced a little bit of just about everything—from women setting me up to get robbed, two brushes with death, a woman that I was real close to being killed, and three women claiming that they were pregnant by me. So me being seriously interested in getting to know a woman or even trusting her would be something short of a miracle.

Before I even get into the rest of this story, the one thing I will say is that I regret that I did not do more constructive things with the extra money, like give it to my mom, save it—but naw, I blew it. I blew it on partying, bad investments and women.

It wasn't all a bust, I did pay for the last

three years of school for one of the trades that I'm certified in, and so that counts. I decided that my long term goal would include going back to school and starting a career and ultimately leaving "the life" completely. Things started to change in my life. I remember my uncle telling me, once you decide to make a change in your life that all things around you would soon change also.

I hadn't given it much thought, but he was right. Things did change and I started noticing. I was in a drought of sorts; problems in the streets, at work, and I hadn't been with a woman in about six months. Yeah a drought, for real!

And then I met her.

My future fiancé and mother of my kids. I remember, I was doing some spring cleaning around my house and needed some detergent so I left and went to the store. I spotted her while shopping and the site of her just had me. She was beautiful.

Her complexion was very smooth, dark chocolate skin, silky long hair, and it was all hers nothing added, just a perm—half way pinned up in a Chinese style ponytail. She wore this shirt —a purple, blue stripped knitted like shirt, dark blue jeans, that hugged every curve of her hips, she stood with a slight knock-kneed stance, and held her hands slightly as if they were used as she spoke in exaggeration to get her point across. Her face had very fine lines and structure, her cheek bones and lips were perfectly shaped a vision of only which models envy and reconstruct themselves to match.

I think she noticed me just about the same time I noticed her, but I was trying to find the right words to say to her and my approach had to be on point. We shared a couple glances for a while as I hesitated while I faked like what was in front of me was something that I wanted to buy.

I studied her face and figure. Yes I was in awe and then the sweetest words came from her mouth *"I think that's sexy to see a man shopping…"*

Now was the time and I was glad she broke the ice too. I hadn't had the language together in my head just yet, didn't want to approach her wrong cause to me she was worth a better conversation than, *"What's your name? Damn you're sexy!"*

So I politely responded, *"Thank you, and would you mind if I take you out sometime, you know anything, maybe dinner and a movie?"*

I was face to face now, looking into her eyes, and damn, her eyes said it all: hurt, anger, love, confusion, chaos, and a need.

"I don't waste my time, money or love," I said. She nodded as if to say she understood. She accepted the offer and we exchanged numbers.

"My name is Karen. Nice to meet you," She said as she turned and I walked away to go to the register.

The crazy thing is that we did not even talk

on the phone or talk to each other period for quite some time after that initial meeting. Then one day out of the blue, she called.

It had been at least two months or so and I didn't remember who it was by then.

She said "*I missed you. I've been thinking about you, it's just been crazy for me lately I still had your number, do you remember who you're talking to?*"

I didn't really, but hey I was dying to find out. She gave me directions to her house.

I met up with her at her apartment building. We sat and talked for a while. She was a hairstylist—she had a client coming over to get their hair done so I left, it did not feel like a waste of time really. Although it was a long trip out to where she lived, it was like going out of town, and during that time in my life it was a much needed break and space to relax.

On about the third visit I found out that she had a little girl. I was on my way out and she told me that she had someone for me to meet, and this little girl came around the corner and said "Hi, *how are you?*"

I was surprised and impressed at the same time, because most women would not waste their time telling you that they had a kid and introduce them to you right off the bat, but I respected that in her. Later, she would say that in order to be with her I had to accept her child as my own.

Now at the time, I had no kids and felt that

I would not want to just come into a kid's life and take ownership of the situation. I would tell her repeatedly, look we can be friends but I will not assume a fatherly role in her daughter's life—that would have to take time.

I left that night and her little girl said *"See you later. You're coming back? You're come back right?"*

That melted my heart. This was what I was missing in my life, a sense of compassion and being needed.

I continued to visit her on a weekly then daily basis. It was my escape from my day to day grind. I took on the role as the only responsible male figure in her daughter's life.

We spent almost every weekend together and it had become the normal thing to do. By year's end, she was pregnant with our first child, but sadly, we lost it some months later. We got the announcement from the doctor, and he was just cold, saying "it's gone" like it wasn't a life and like it didn't mean anything.

Shortly after that she was pregnant again. I remember the second pregnancy was a great bonding time for us both. I would do just about anything for Karen and her daughter, spoiling them with gifts and making sure that they did not want for anything. I had taken on the role of head of the household even paying bills that were not mine. I had lived on a very busy strip where anything could pop off at any moment and it normally would. I had moved there to pay cheaper rent because anywhere else would've cost an arm and a leg—definitely, a "you get what you pay for" type of spot.

My life was changing, school and a new baby on the way and it forced me to put things into perspective. I couldn't go on trying to juggle my dual lifestyles any longer, and it was evident to me that I had to make a choice. I knew that eventually my side hustle had to come to an end, because I ran the risk of getting locked up or worse, killed. So I had a plan. I started working a full time job and slowly got out of the life and put money away for the future.

Rocky Road

Our relationship was like any other relationship, for young adults still trying to find their way. We were full of disagreements, mistrust and no guidance.

I never really took the time to just sit back and really look at our relationship and how we interacted with one another. I just went with the flow of things. And after my daughter was born, the honeymoon was over.

I understood that most if not all women go through some sort of post partum stress after having a baby—it happens, but this was a whole different case. During the course of the relationship there were signs that I had ignored or just felt that I could work through, disagreements are normal and our relationship was no stranger to those.

My daughter had eczema. Doctor visits were frequent. Being a new parent myself I took a great interest in finding out what this condition was and do whatever I could to help out and to make sure my little girl was ok. She would scratch at her face until it bled, and from doctor visits to doctor visits it just seemed that it had gotten worse. By that time, being a bystander was no longer an option for me. So I asked Karen *"do you think that you can get a second opinion, because it seems like nothing that the doctor gives her works?*"

That set off a whirlwind of emotions and accusations that I would not live down. Apparently, asking her to get a second opinion was the same as telling her she was not a good mother. I started to hear that comment more and more when it came to my input on either my daughter's condition or any type of parenting issue period for that matter.

If I understood one thing about Karen, it's that she had a rough childhood, teenage years and even early adulthood. She had been through a lot and as I learned later, I could not go back and correct or solve her issues. I just tried to deal with them the best way I knew how and love her. It seemed like I was fighting an uphill battle and at every turn it seemed like this relationship was doomed to fail. The only thing we seemed to have in common anymore was the kids.

I tried my best to show her that whatever she went through in her life that I didn't care, and I would love her and be there for her and our kids.

"*I am not that guy!*"

I wondered why she had this notion in her head that she would always revert back to whenever we had a disagreement on anything related to our kids.

"*Men aren't supposed to do . . . they don't care about that.*"

But she was wrong.

I was that man who cared and did do my

job. Unlike a lot of guys I knew who would run away and not take care of their kids. So why did I get all the blame? I struggled with this issue all through our relationship. I could have been the type of man she was used to and just up and run away from my responsibilities, but that was not me. I stayed for her and the kids.

The reasons that I stayed, I think came from deep within me. I never really had a stable life growing up with both a mother and father in the household working together to raise and take care of their kids. Yes we had our mother, my brother and sister and I, but we needed a man in the house too. And not just every now and then, but a stable figure in the house.

When I was 10 and my brother was 12, my mother told us both, "*I can't teach you how to be a man, I'm a woman. So you're gonna have to figure that out for yourself.*"

I guess I wanted the best for my kids no matter what, to have a father in the house at any cost, it was not stable at all but at least I was there—was my thought.

We were divided on a lot of things at times, and we struggled with roles in our household. I was the one providing what the family needed and she had to play her role in taking care of the kids and so on and so on. Meanwhile, while we were still trying to figure it all out, Karen had become pregnant again, and this time we had a boy.

Life was still crazy for us both, but the time

spent during her pregnancy was the most peaceful time we had. It was funny actually—while normally we had a life of pure confusion when she was pregnant it seemed like all the drama stopped. That would not last for long though, because outside of that we were still "oil and water."

Young and dumb are what I attribute that to, but then again some people never change. They are who they are and nothing seemed to change her ways. We had gone through battles and battles over and over again and it was wearing on my spirit. By the time my son was a year old I had asked Karen to marry me, which was unrealistic.

Yes, us getting married!

We could not agree on anything and everything had become my fault. I remember her always saying *"I can't stand you; I want to do things for myself, and you're controlling me!"* And me thinking: fine then. Go ahead and go back to work so you can do for yourself and don't have to worry about me controlling you.

The problem was, for years I had taken care of the family, but in the beginning I was spoiling everybody. I was looking toward the future again and now, being that we had more mouths to feed and other bills, we needed to be more conservative. Control was an issue because she did not have any, so she thought. I had most of the money which went to taking care of the household and at times I would treat myself to something new. It's not like I didn't treat her or the kids to something new, they were covered. But of course money became an issue among the myriad of other things.

When it was all said and done, I had bought three engagement rings and still hadn't solved either one of our problems.

We were headed for destruction. I started looking into other options by that time. We had gotten to the point where there was no peace in the house. I remember coming home and all I would hear is her fusing about something. I had become displeased with my situation all together. I was in a place I did not want to be anymore, the woman that I was giving my life to, was not seeing my value and worth. I'm taking care of her and the kids, doing what I have to do and getting no respect and I was done with it.

The other factor was she dealt with low self-esteem, which in hindsight; I could not correct or save her from herself. Plenty of times she would lash out and even pulled a knife on me over a disagreement. I had to decide for my sake and the children what was best for all of us. I looked into buying a new place and leaving and letting her and the kids stay where they were. During that time, it seemed like everything around me was falling down, I made a bad investment and lost a lot of money and then the house that we were renting went into foreclosure. As if it could not get any worse!

We had gone through therapy; tried living together, I had given up the life, raising kids together wasn't working. Now stuck in this position we are back to square one and forced to make it work. The last option was to move together. Hell, we still loved each other, so why not try to make it work again. Her friend had moved from Maryland to Atlanta, so she had the idea for us to move to there. So that's what we did.

The move to Atlanta was going to be our new beginning.

We did not know the city. We could get a fresh start and just maybe things would change for us. The saying *"You are who you are, you've changed your layers, but underneath you're the same"* held a lot of weight with our relationship because the more things changed they stayed the same.

We settled in the Atlanta area and I got a job with the apartment complex where we wound up staying. I went back to school for massage therapy. I figured that I had to create more avenues for revenue being that I had a party of four to take care of and I had always been good with my hands.

Karen did not like my choice, but I had to think about our future. I had to deal with her insecurities—again. She was so used to me being around and now I was busy with work and school, but she had other things on her mind. We were doing well as long as I was home. But it all started again; with her trying to catch me in the act or prove that I was cheating on her.

I worked a lot of overtime with the apartment complex on call and also going to school at night, she thought I was not working but out cheating. In the past I would leave the house whenever we got into heated arguments, so my time away was left up to speculation. I just needed time away.

This particular night I had gotten a call from her and she asked where I was and I told her by the trash dump throwing out trash. I drove back to the school after her call to pick up my books. I was on call and left school to fix a resident's A/C unit, after which I headed back to school which was only down the street. I picked up my books and then drove back home and as soon as I get to my turn I noticed that Karen and her girlfriend were following me.

Once in the complex I stopped and got out of my car. She jumped out yelling, like she had caught me red handed. She yelled and all I could do is laugh to myself because it was just crazy.

Pause.

I had gone back to school to put together another way to earn money, since for so long I had been the sole provider and we had a growing family and now needed two incomes to survive. It had really gotten to a point where I let her know that with the way things were going she really needed to manage how she spent money a little bit better. I was not bringing in the same amount of money anymore and I was feeling the pinch and she needed to help out anyway that she could.

She had a talent in doing hair, so I encouraged her to start something on the side and I would support her and help her get business until we could both come up and afford to get a shop of our own. We had always had two different ways of thought when it came to progress. She made excuses for why she couldn't and I always had a plan for us to achieving success together. I was pushing for us to try and work together and really meant it. For instance I left a check for her one day so she could go on the internet and purchase business cards for her side gig of doing hair. The check never made it to the post office and she showed no signs of wanting to start her own side business doing hair, or anything else.

We had been together for quite some time and all the talking in the world was not gonna change anything in her mind at this point. We had gone through our highest highs and lowest lows in the relationship and now it was at a complete standstill and not productive at all. I decided that I would not let her insecurities get in the way of the priorities: taking care of our family and keeping a roof over our heads. So now, not only did I work my full time job and go to school, but I also did work on the side, fixing cars body work, heating and ac replacement repairs and service work, whatever I needed to, to make some extra money.

She was not enthusiastic about it at all. In fact, the more I did the more it seemed to make her angry. But I couldn't just sit around and besides, who else was gonna help out to pay these bills. Not her. She had made it clear, "*I ain't nobody's slave, I almost died having these kids for you.*"

I decided that we needed to have a business relationship and work together; no longer could she reap the benefits in this relationship without helping in some way. She had made up in her mind what she was not gonna do and most nights, I was left with dirty dishes to wash after working all day and going to school at night. So I continued on doing odd jobs and going to school, making money on the side, my name had gotten around, and if you needed your car fixed and for a reasonable price I was the one to come see.

I was approached that morning to come take a look at a car. It was similar to the one that I had at the time, a Ford Crown Victoria. I was familiar with the repair, so we made arrangements for the young lady to drop off her car and I would work on it. She and I along with her boyfriend talked about the problems that she was having, the shocks sounded like they were bad and the suspension was sagging up front. No problem. I knew that the control arm bushings had worn out and normally they would split and your wheel could fall off, or worse.

I made a list of the deficiencies while under the car. The gentleman had left the car with me and let me know that his girlfriend would be back later to retrieve the keys and pay me so I could get the parts and fix the car. I went through the car's undercarriage with a fine tooth comb, noting the problems and most important issues, the girlfriend showed up while I was under the car and began to ask me questions about the car. Once I was done under the car I came out to introduce myself and go over the cost of parts and repair.

And then it happened!

I turned around and my baby mama and her girlfriend pulled into the parking lot; she jumped out and motioned for me to come to her and I motioned back that I was busy with the car up in the air, but her face said that she was pissed. When it was all said and done I had worked on the lady's car for free. Baby mama had made a scene and scared the lady away, which was bad for my business and my pockets.

I went inside and that's when the fight began. I was at the counter washing my hand when she started throwing candles, bottles, flowers whatever she could find.

She started punching me and pulling my hair, yelling and just kept hitting me. I kept telling her to stop. The kids were there watching this all happening and I wanted it to stop. I grabbed her and picked her up and slammed her to the ground and she let go. I told her that was it. I was done with us in that fit of rage.

This had been our first real physical fight where there had been actual punches thrown, it had gone against everything that I stood for. I never wanted to physically fight a woman. I had come close before in throwing blows with a woman but I would just grab and hold on. And I did just that, grabbed her and held on. I could not bring myself to close my fist and hit a woman, and at this point I was not gonna start.

For the rest of the day after that, I stayed clear of her. I figured that when we cooled off, then we could talk about what had happened and discuss our future. I was just in heavy thought that night when I went to bed; so many things were said and done that day that I figured that I would sleep with the door locked. She slept in our oldest daughter's room and the kids all slept together.

I really thought about what would be the topic of discussion and what would be the outcome, but it had become a hopeless situation. I had rededicated myself to this woman so many times before, and still the same results. I looked at myself at this time and asked the hard questions of myself, was I being fair? Was I doing all that I could to keep this family together? And, what were the things that I may have done or doing to cause us to have such a huge problem with trust?

I realized that we were fighting a losing battle, so it was time to make up my mind and do it fast. I went to sleep, and then heard a knock on the door. It was my son, so I opened the door and let him in, shut the door again and we both got back in the bed and went to sleep.

About five minutes passed and I heard a

hard knocking on the door. It was her. She yelled while banging on the door, *"What are you doing in there with my son and why is the door locked?"*

I had the door locked to insure that she was not gonna act on her earlier threat, better safe than sorry. I did not want my neighbors to call the police because they heard her yelling at the top of her lungs and banging on the door. We were in the wrong place for that. Just earlier that week, police in our county had served a "no knock entry" on a home they had suspected of drug activity, resulting in them shooting a 90 something year-old lady. I was not trying to go down that road, especially with a domestic issue here in Georgia. I'm a young black male and will not get the benefit of a doubt. They would just shoot me too. She had threatened earlier that day that she would call the police and tell them that I had a gun in the house and that would not be a pretty sight. I wanted to try and keep the peace.

She just kept yelling for me to open up the door, and then said, *"If you're not molesting him why do you have the door locked?"* At this point I couldn't believe she would say something like that. It was just crazy!

I opened the door and she rushed in to get my son out of the bed. He was calling out to me *"Daddy, Daddy"*

She said *"He ain't you're damn daddy!"* That right there just took me over the edge. I wanted nothing more to do with this woman. I was crushed and all the doubt, anger and frustrations of years had come to the surface. I was seeing red.

I was now really contemplating beating her up, doing some type of harm and even murder. I had never felt that way about her before. I felt shame, embarrassment, felt like a damn fool and like I had wasted my time—just to come to this. I had to get away from her, get away. I left the house that night to clear my mind. That night would be the catalyst to a new way of thinking, and change me forever.

Advice From an Unlikely Source

In my haste and hurry to just get out and get some air, I wasn't watching my speed as I drove down the street and was pulled over by a police officer.

When the officer approached the car, all I was thinking about in my head was that she had called them and that I was going to jail. The officer came up to the driver's side window and asked me if everything was ok?

He was not nervous, as most are or demanding of seeing my license and registration, he just wanted to know if everything was ok. But that was short lived; he started in on me about how he had a disdain for "niggers."

I answered him with "*me too, I hate niggers.*"

He looked at me as if he had a loss for words. "*I love black people, white people, Chinese people, all people but I hate niggers,*" I said. "*Don't you know you have niggers in every race?*"

Right then he paused and turned his head, like a puzzled dog. By then I noticed that he had gotten out of his police cruiser and was standing next to my car with his gun out. Then he asked me again staring directly into my eyes, "*What's wrong with you?*"

So I told him what had just happened and

expressed to him that I had too much to lose and did not want to have them show up and it going down the way I feared it might. I asked him what my options were, and asked him to put his self in my shoes. What would he do?

We spoke about the situation for about 30 minutes and he advised me to act first, because in Georgia I would not stand a chance, especially if they had to come out on a domestic dispute and the mention of a gun, abuse and kids were involved. With a plain face, looking me dead in my eyes, after I asked him what he thought would happen if that scenario had played out, he answered "You would probably get locked up, or worse, be killed." He added that he took it to be a serious threat, being that a mention of a gun being involved that he would not take any chances.

"Ahh I enjoy bussing niggers heads," He really did not care for niggers, and if it was up to him they could all die! I sat there as he went on his trip down memory lane as he told me about a similar situation, but the suspect was white and a friend of his. Someone that he knew had been caught up in the same situation and the arresting officers took the woman's side of the story and almost killed the guy. Later on he was found innocent of any charges.

I sat there and wondered why would a white officer that is not shy at all about his disdain for "niggers" would give me advice on saving myself from the law. He told me, from that night on to record every conversation and make a police report right now.

"Go up to the station and file tonight. I know about what all do up north, you don't talk like them niggers down here so you from up north right?"

I told him yes.

"Well, that 'no snitching bullshit, don't work down here. You're in Georgia now." He told me to file a report so that I would have a leg to stand on.

"Start keeping copies of everything." Basically, he told me that I had no chance in the world for justice if I did not have concrete evidence of what was going on so it would not just be her word against mine and/or the officer's boot up side my head.

I stayed out that night, got me a room at a local hotel and just sat back and relaxed. This thing that I was going through was really stressing me out and I was on edge and did not need to be in the house because that would definitely be trouble. She kept calling me wanting to talk or rather argue with me.

"What are you doing? ...Why don't you just come back and talk about it? ...You using what I said as a scapegoat to do what you want to do! ...Oh when shit gets thick you want to walk away, you ain't no man!"

Actually I just wanted to just get away and not have to deal with this shit and get myself in trouble. So, I slept in peace and quiet that night.

The next morning, I got up early and went back to the apartment. Everyone was asleep, so I took a shower, put on my work clothes and left. I worked where we lived, so it was convenient to just get up and step outside the door and be at work.

Her girlfriend's mother was the head of management for the apartment complex (which would later become a whole separate issue). See there was a lot of talk going on with the manager's daughter, since she and my baby moms were cool. She always had her two cents to add to any disagreement that we had, and made our business her business. I spoke with her mother, the apartment manager, and she assured me that her daughter was all wrapped up in what was going on in my house, also she was supposed to be my daughter's godmother of sorts and she had been advised her to stay out of it.

From the night before with me going to the police department to file, they sent a car to the complex to follow-up. I spoke to the officer and she asked me if I wanted to press charges at that point which would be "simple assault and cruelty to minors, three counts." I didn't want to press charges but just to keep it on file. The officer gave me a copy of the paperwork and I went back to work. I had to cover my ass and it seemed to have made a couple of people mad.

Enough...Turning Point

The next day while I was away at lunch I called my kids' mother and reminded her to go and pick our daughter up from the bus stop

"Make sure you get Mya from the bus stop ok?"

"No, you make sure you get her from the bus stop," she said.

But I was nowhere close to the property to do so. She was in the apartment and just a short walk away from the front gate—her excuse was that my son was sleeping, and that they could just take my daughter back to the school.

So, I asked her again to go pick her up, and all she kept saying was that she was not going to get my son up and go get our daughter from the bus stop.

I didn't think that she would do something like that, but I got a call from one of the ladies at the rental office. *"I have someone right here that looks just like you in my office."*

Where is her mother?

"I don't know, I heard someone knocking when I was on my way out to lunch, and I wasn't gonna answer the door, but she just kept knocking louder and when I came to the door it was her."

My heart just dropped to my stomach. How could she just leave our 5-year old at the bus stop on a busy street? I still didn't know the area that well and neither did she. I'm glad that my daughter had enough sense to go to the rental office and knock on the door, who knows what could have happened. I rushed back to the property and kept trying to call my kid's mother but did not get an answer. I picked my daughter up from the office. I just looked at her and she looked back.

"*Are you ok boo boo?*"

"*Yeah,*" she said.

I took her home and I asked Karen, "*how come you did not go get her from the bus stop?*"

Her reply, "*you got her now right.*"

We started arguing, and Mya started to cry. Then and there I was done. I know I said it before, but this was my last straw.

I got to work that next morning and my manager asked about the incident that went on the day before in the parking lot. I explained what happened and that I was going to protect my best interests—meaning not ending up in jail and filing a police report. She did not agree with my reasoning, but I had to protect myself, so I filed. I knew that she did not know the full story or even know about the years that we spent together and that now was the breaking point of our relationship and that I had enough, but she was going to be biased because of her daughter and her relationship with my baby momma.

I made the report that morning, left on my lunch break and finished filing with the court and by the close of business the next day I was fired.

The manager had something to say about a

customer compliant, but I knew that it was much deeper than that. I had filed the paperwork and it was served the next morning, with two parts, for legitimacy and child support. I wanted to do the right thing by my kids and for the relationship. They still needed a father in their lives and this relationship needed some kind of checks and balances.

I made the best decision that I could make and stood up and became a man in the eyes of the law. See I say "in the eyes of the law," because I was already doing what a man was supposed to do, but no one else knew or really cared. I made this decision because we had a verbal agreement that we would conduct the business of family this way for years but that contract now was null and void.

Not only was I made a fool of, but leaving my future in her hands would have been downright crazy. It had become a power struggle for quite some time in our household. She would gripe about control all the time, "*So you feel that you can just do whatever you want with your money because you go out and work?*

Uh yeah, but the bottom line is that I did for them with my money 100 percent, and at times it would be a power struggle that was so damn pointless and immature. Whatever happened in our relationship from this point on, at least I could be sure that my kids would have everything that they needed.

When I went to the courthouse to apply for

legitimacy, the clerk advised me to have the paperwork served to my kid's mother in order for the court to acknowledge that both parties were aware of the proceedings.

The next morning the Sheriff showed up at the door and served her with the paperwork. She was upset and kept yelling at me about why I did what I did, but plain and simple I had to take charge of this situation and my life and kid's life.

I was planning to deal with however the situation played out, either share time with the kids, paying for a place to stay for them—it didn't matter I don't know what to really do at that point. So it was no surprise that she would go back home and I prepared myself to deal with either a long distance relationship with my kids or just moving back home and taking care of them there.

This is where it started—with the letter on the door that I spoke of earlier.

I walked in and there was complete silence. I checked our oldest daughter's room first, then the kids' room.

Nothing.

No signs of them anywhere.

All of her daughter's clothes, her clothes and my son's clothes were gone, except Mya's.

As I turned around to go outside, I found the note on the door.

"Please pay the electric bill, and pick up Mya. She is over Tonya's house."

Tonya was her best friend and the one who,

when we were having problems in Maryland, suggested that we move to Atlanta to start over.

Karen had left and gone back to Maryland, and left my daughter which was crazy—she has three kids and she leaves one?

I went to Tonya's house to pick up Mya, my emotions going up and down, wondering why she did this and how was Mya feeling.

I knocked on the door and Tonya answered the door and there stood Mya, I could tell that she was crying. Without saying a word, I grabbed her hand and we walked home.

Mya told me that she wanted to go with them and her mom told her that she had to stay here with me, *"Daddy I wanted to go but she told me that I could not go, and why?"*

At that point I had no answer for her because honestly, I couldn't answer it for myself either.

Why would she do this?

That night I must have called her more than a hundred times, left message after message and got no response. Mya cried for two hours that night until she finally fell asleep. I cried while she slept, watching her taking each breath as I thought about our loss. I thought about our life together back from the day that my daughter was born, the day my son was born and everything in between.

At the time it was a painful situation, but it was also a damn good release, a weight on my shoulders that was lifted.

The next day I dropped Mya off to school and went back to the courthouse. I wanted to check with the court and find out what was the next step for me. I spoke with the clerk's office again and told them about my situation and that my kid was abandoned by her mother. They advised me to file with the court—again. I filed and in short, they could not believe me. Basically they really did not know if the mother had left the state or not and that I did not have any more rights to my daughter than she had. I had already filed for the child support and everything else so all I could do was continue the required paperwork. I was advised to get a lawyer.

The next week I signed up for a 5 hour seminar for divorcing parents. I remember going into the police department to attend the seminar, not knowing what to expect, other than it was gonna be a long day. I arrived early, and sat in the car.

I had mixed emotions. This was the first step in securing a future for me and my kids, knowing that the road would be rough and I needed backup to show the court system that I was serious about my role as a man and a father.

I looked around and saw that I was the only car, other than a few police cars in the parking lot. After awhile, cars started filing in and they sat in their cars just like me. Maybe they were anxiously awaiting the results of this seminar and becoming that much closer to some kind of closure, peace of mind and direction from this point on.

I remember just looking at all of the cars in that lot wondering, what brought them here? Would I hear anyone with the same story, or would it just be a class full of actual divorcing parents. I felt out of place because I was not ever married, but had to take the class as a "divorcing parent." People started to line up at the door and like a call to lunch, all of the car doors opened and everyone started their trek to the door. I got out and stood in line.

I was a cloud of nervousness. People just standing around, looking at each other and separate conversations were going on. Some laughing and joking about having to be there. There was a lady and a man there, seemed like they were a couple. They had come together and it seemed like they were actual divorcing parents, separating from each other. I learned later that they were divorcing from their spouses and were actually together. They were the funny couple of that day, had everybody cracking up, which lightened the mood.

During the class, we had two instructors who gave the outline of the seminar and personal experiences and tools to deal with the separation and how to deal with the relationships moving forward, between mother, father and kids and even how to deal with other folks that wanted to have a negative influence in your transition.

I did hear from other folks that had it rougher than me. I just wanted to do the right thing by my kids and avoid most of the bumps that they were going through. I took in all that the seminar had to offer, they gave us some contact information and a road map for the path ahead— even a very helpful book that dealt with dispute resolution that turned out to be a resource that I would revisit later on in my journey. It was a start. Plus it showed the courts that I was on the right track.

After the seminar was done, they gave us information on the next step, which involved more of the other parties input, i.e. mediation. There were many hoops to jump through in order to start the process for legitimating and it was mandatory to take this class and meditation between both parties. I was supposed to get an answer from my kid's mother and setup mediation, even if it had to be separate—I take it in Georgia and she takes it in Maryland.

That week I went in for an interview for the local cable company. I got the job and started the next day. I loved the working hours, because it allowed me to drop my daughter off at school and get off in time to pick her up. It was perfect.

I switched my classes to nights and dropped Mya off at my baby momma's friend's house. She extended her help to me to watch her at night while I went to school. That was short lived because baby momma called her and told her not to help me out, so I found another person to watch her while I went to school. All the while, I kept petitioning the court, filing paperwork and following the process, my petition for abandonment, deprivation was denied. I kept getting the same response, but had proof that she had left the state. Even the school and doctor's office were aware of it but still…nothing. The court had received a letter from Karen, stating her new address and still I had no recourse or leg to stand on. I was still without any rights.

In the letter Karen told the court that she had moved back to Maryland and gave them her new address. That was proof enough that my daughter was left with me and that Karen no longer resided in the state of Georgia. It seemed like I could not get a break, but I kept pressing on, writing letters and redoing the necessary paperwork.

Mya's Trial

Although I was not making any headway in the courts, I still had my daughter.

Mya had a field trip and I signed up as a chaperone we went to the petting zoo. It was a lot of fun actually. We saw all types of animals, the kids played in a maze, and at the end we went on a hay ride. There was a peacock there that kept making a loud sound all day long. You could hear it making its call "Waaahhhhh Waaaahhhh!"

We sat down and watched a show in a barn sitting on hand made benches, and the kids received small pumpkins to take home. At the end of the trip we stopped to have lunch and afterwards we went over to the last set of animals, a dirty mule, a llama and a goat.

I made sure I kept an eye on Mya to keep her from touching the animals because they seemed a little off, but kids are gonna be kids and before we left, she put her hand on the llama and I hurried up and had her wash her hands.

The next morning I woke up to low whimpering and hearing the water running in Mya's bathroom.

When I went in to see what the problem was, she was at the sink scrubbing her hands. I noticed that she had bumps on a couple of her fingers which seem to come up on top and in the palm part of her hand. The bumps were in clusters and they were white with a bubble like shapes. She said that they itched like crazy.

I took her into the doctors that morning and the doctor could not diagnosis for certain what it was at the time. So he sent us home with a prescription.

By that night, other bumps had shown up on other parts of her body, her face, underarms, forearms, elbows, stomach, legs, back and even her feet. I took her into the emergency room and by the time we arrived she was in a lot of pain. She said that it felt like something was under her skin and the doctors there was not much help. They guessed that it was Hand, Foot and Mouth disease.

We went to the Health Department, I notified her school and questioned if there was an outbreak at school of other kids being sick. At the Health Department they thought that it might be a strain of the disease that causes chicken pox but really weren't too sure either. She was vaccinated as a precaution. I took her back to her primary care physician the next morning and he said that it shared some properties of the HFMD but also shared some symptoms of MRSA, and around that time that was the big scare going around staph infections and that she could have a mix of both.

He advised me to keep her out of school until the blisters and pain went away, keep her medicated and suggested I keep her home from school. I had to take off from work. I tried calling her mother to let her know what was going on with her, but once I did get in touch with her I was surprised what she had to say.

"I have moved on and don't have time"

I told her Mya was sick she was like *"…and well."*

Really? How you just gonna say that?

She replied with, *"Well I might as well treat it like another adoption and say fuck her!"*

How could a mother just off her daughter like that? I knew that she really had a problem. My daughter asked about her mother about two more times after that day and then she had become a moot point. She was hurting physically and mentally and I just filled the void and did my best to care for her. Her sickness was a rough road and even the diagnosis was too. The doctor couldn't really give a name for it—he just kept prescribing medications. Mya's condition just kept getting worse and he could not make heads or tails of her illness.

I stayed up most nights during her ordeal, so many nights up just holding my daughter trying to comfort the pains and reassure her that it would be all right. Her illness started to affect her appetite. She did not eat that much and the food that she did eat she would vomit later. We visited her doctor's office again for a checkup and to see what progress had been made. The doctor suggested that we go to a dermatologist and he referred us to one that he knew.

We met with the dermatologist that Friday and she ordered blood work, an allergy test and a biopsy to be done to narrow down the possibilities. I took pictures of Mya and all the areas that had the blisters, it was also included in the report that the dermatologist put together. The dermatologist detailed the areas on a model where the blisters were present and called them legions and kept track of the process of healing.

The medicine started to take effect somewhere in the third week and we started to see signs of improvement. However she still had an acute respiratory issue. The illness had driven her immune system way down and she did not have an appetite. This meant I had to keep up with giving her liquids and foods that she could hold down. Needless to say this was a very trying time in both of our lives; she had lost her mother, sister and baby brother, and now dealing with this illness that was just taking everything out of her poor little body.

I felt somewhat helpless at moments and did most of my hard crying after she fell asleep in my arms every night. My tears were for her, she was so weak and not knowing if this was going to get any worse really took a toll on me emotionally. On the other end I knew she was torn apart, she kept asking me if she was loved.

"Why did mommy leave me? She don't love me anymore?"

Week four, and now we are getting

somewhere, she is healing well but there is still a lot of scaring from the blisters and still some of the bumps remain on her fingers and toes. We met with the dermatologist that Friday and she ordered yet more blood work, an allergy test and a biopsy to be done to narrow down the possibilities.

With all of the things that my little girl had been through she had to endure another traumatic event, and that was the biopsy. The doctor had to get a piece of her skin so that they could run tests on it and determine what type of illness it could be.

The nurse came into the room and introduced herself and asked me to help her, "*I need for you to hold her for me please. It will hurt a lot so I need for her to be really still...*"

She told Mya that she would use the tool to take out a little bit of her skin and that it was gonna hurt a little, then asked her if it was alright to start now. Mya just nodded. The nurse assured her that "*This might hurt so please stay as still as possible...*"

I sat there trying to be strong for her, because I knew how much pain that she was in and how much more pain she would be in after them taking a piece of her skin and not even giving her something beforehand. No anesthetic to numb her before cutting a piece of her skin out.

I looked at the tool that the nurse took out to use. It looked like a cross between a single hole punch and a finger nail file. I held onto Mya's hand as I braced for the reaction of my daughter when the tool pierced her skin, all three of us took a deep breath. The nurse pushed the one side of the tool up against her elbow then began to press. I tell you… I just held my breath and winced. The nurse stood there wincing herself as she cut the piece of meat out of my daughter's arm.

I looked up and my daughter's face was expressionless, she didn't even wince. I could not believe it! My daughter did not utter a word, me and the nurse both was surprised. I wanted to cry at that very moment, my daughter; so small and weak had soldiered through the most trying time of her young life, being without her siblings, a mother gone and now having to endure this pain had not flinched!

My heart and mind were heavy. I mourned for her, anguished over the thought of what she had to be going through; she gave me strength and courage. I had seen God's presence at that moment in my daughter's eyes. The nurse all in amazement kept asking my daughter *"Are you ok? Oh my God! She did not even flinch, what a tough little girl!"* When my daughter answered the nurse, she said *"it didn't hurt."*

I hadn't worked for a while now, and money was running low, and I had just started the new job and my insurance had not yet taken affect yet. The dermatologist suggested light treatment to help heal Mya's skin and it would cost $1,200. I explained to the doctor that I did not have the money and at that time they were not accepting my type of insurance, so the doctor did it for free. It was a blessing!

The process took another two weeks and during that time she had my daughter undergo light therapy to help heal the wounds. Mya would go into a machine that looked like a tanning booth for about 10 minutes per session. She thought it was cool because she got to wear sunglasses. After all the tests came back, it was inconclusive as either HFMD or MRSA but an infection that triggered severe dermatitis, which may have had a glimpse of one or two types of similar diseases. She was doing better but not out of the woods yet, the doctor suggested that she continue taking the medication until everything had totally cleared up. Mya's appetite had come back and she was back to eating just about everything in sight!

Paper Trail

This time in our lives took a toll on my time at school also. I had to miss about two and half months of classes and since most of them comprised of hands on course work, my courses were marked incomplete for that time to be made up at a later date. I am forever grateful for my classmates and instructors for being there for me during that time in my life and they stepped up to the plate in a major way. Whenever I needed help with my daughter while I went to work there was always someone who lent a hand to help.

Once Mya's health was better and she was off to school and I was back to work. I continued to petition the court and follow the process; to see what my rights were, the next step that I had to take to ensure that it was documented that my daughter was in my sole custody and that her mother had just wrote her off and wanted nothing to do with her.

The process was a long and tedious one, and all of the documents were a bit confusing because the wording had to be spelled out in a certain way. But I was on a mission and with little to no resources left, I took on the hard learning curve of the legal system.

In my off times, I researched all of the legal formalities and processes over again after being rejected by the clerk's office, determined to get it right. I don't know how many times I visited the clerk's office and how many times I presented the proper paperwork time and time again, but there was one thing that I was missing and that was the wording—it had to be worded and drawn out the right way for them to accept it and not only the wording but the proper paperwork.

I looked on the net for the local county government website and read through their processes. I downloaded and printed off any documents that related to my case, and I filled them all out and turned them into the clerk's office. The clerk advised me again to get a lawyer, and in my mind I felt that no one else would have the same passion that I had to get this case finished so I stayed on the grind. My overall mind set was that when I did get a lawyer that I would save him the time, cause by then all he would have to do is show up to court.

The issue that I was dealing with was that even though she was my blood daughter I still had to wait on the process of legitimating. I had my name on her birth certificate and still you mean to tell me that was not enough? It just seemed that I was doing all of this leg work for nothing. So I finally gave in, and decided to go see a lawyer.

I made an appointment with a local attorney and she had given me some very important information that I had overlooked during my time researching the process—something to do with "proper jurisdiction." The statute outlined that for one, in layman's terms: minor children were; considered under the jurisdiction of the county in which they resided for more than six months, and neither parent could take a minor child out of the jurisdiction of the court without consent and/or during the process of an ongoing legal process: i.e. my petition for child support and legitimacy.

This was great news for me because I had served her the paperwork and during that time we both had to answer to the court process, but she didn't. I left the lawyer's office now armed with more information; I found the document and submitted it into the clerk's office. Even though the law had stated that there was a violation, it still did not do well for me for the purpose of legitimacy. I needed something else, and unbeknownst to me I would receive help from yet another unlikely source.

Dealing with the clerk's office I was hitting a brick wall. My kids' mother was against my decision to legitimize them and voluntary put myself on child support—mostly because this act took the control away from her and put it squarely into the hands of the court, which I had no problem with since I was getting nowhere with her.

She entered a letter into the clerk's office via mail which helped my situation out dramatically. In the first part of the letter she acknowledged that I was the father of my kids. *Yes just what I needed!* She also tried to make other demands in that letter, for instance demanding that I pay child support, which I had already enrolled myself. She requested that I not be able to see the kids unless I paid her child support. The best part of the letter was when she explained that I as a father was abusive and unemployed at the time of her leaving and that we both agreed to her leaving with two out of the three kids, leaving my daughter behind.

Reading this you have to wonder, "What the hell is wrong with this picture?"

Ok let's look at this for real...

She would knowingly leave her daughter with an "abusive" father who was unemployed? That is crazy! She went on to say that she did not want her child to feel any adornment [sic]. I know, I spelled it wrong but that's how it was typed, because she was once a child who had been abandoned.

In the end she pleaded to the courts that she did not want her child to feel any adornment. I figured that she and her loud mouth girlfriend came up with this letter, cause it screamed, "Two dumb asses came up with this letter."

For the record, the word adornment means to embellish or make beautiful. She didn't want my daughter to be embellished or made beautiful for being left in the care of her loving father.

Wow!

Later I received a phone call from her girlfriend, who left a message on my answering machine, calling me all sorts of names and trying to jump out there with me. I recorded it and used it as motivation and later as evidence. That part would become my biggest asset in this case— recording everything and formulating a plan from all the information that I gathered. I believed that what I was doing was good, noble and righteous— just trying to take care of my kids.

Thief in the Day

We started to settle into life a little better, just me and Mya.

Our schedule was set: drop her off, go to work, get off and pick her up from the bus stop. At work, I learned that one of my baby momma's classmates worked with me and she had stayed in contact with her. I tried to keep conversation with her to a minimum. She would let me know when she had spoken to her as if she was reporting to me but all the while I knew really reporting back to her about what's going on with me at work. I saw her angle and was not going to play into it. I just had to just keep pressing on with the business at hand and do my work and take care of my daughter.

It was the turn of the year and it would be the first of the birthdays that I would miss. My son was turning three and I had no idea where he lived. I was nearing the end of all the paperwork needed to start the process and my total packet was going to be submitted by week's end. I was getting closer to securing a court date until the rug was pulled from up under me.

It was the weekend; we caught the new Simpson's movie at a new theater that just opened up. It was so new; we were the only ones at the movie. We went shopping for clothes and shoes that day too. It had been a long time since we had an outing and just had time to relax and enjoy ourselves. She was no longer sickly but still taking medicine and we had the cloud of depression lifted. Sunday we went to service early and stayed for both the morning and evening services. We heard a good word, "Persistence Pays Off" and I was praying for strength to last through the process.

Monday morning, like any other morning, we got ready, I dropped her off at school gave her a big hug, kissed her on the forehead told her I loved her and headed to work. Traffic was crazy and for some reason my car was acting up. It stalled out on me twice while I was headed to work, about 60 miles from school to work and I got to work with just minutes to spare.

It was one of those days that just kept me so busy that I almost ran over the time, I looked up and it was 2 pm. I left work and got caught in traffic on my way, then I got a call from my babysitter. She said that Mya did not get off the bus today. I told her to go to her school and check there.

She called me back once she got to her school and told me that she wasn't there either. My heart dropped and I started to panic.

I started driving on the side of the highway, trying my best to get to my daughters school as fast as I could—all the while on the phone with local authorities. I called the FBI, requested that they place a missing child report. I get a call on the other line from a blocked number and it's my kid's mother. She tells me *"No need to pick Mya up from school today, ha ha I got her."*

I told her stop playing and bring her back because she did not care about her, but she was already gone. I found out later once I got to the school that she had signed her out earlier that morning once I had dropped her off—so she was well out of the state before I found out that she was missing.

After six months she comes back out of the blue and takes her away from me! I had tried to change the information at the school, but because I did not have a court order to do so I could not block her from taking my daughter.

The school did not even give me the courtesy of calling me as I had noted in the emergency information. I called CPS in Maryland and filed a report with them, they took down all of the information I gave them. They let me know that there was little that they could do, but when they got a chance and an address on them they would go and check up on the kids.

I kept in contact with CPS in Maryland, practically on a weekly basis, but still no progress. This almost broke my spirit. I was about to just call it quits and throw in the towel.

I just could not believe that this was happening.

I got really depressed. Thoughts of just

doing something really dumb kept coming up in my head. I was angry and felt cheated and felt like striking out. I struggled all week long to channel my energy to something good.

I keep calling and texting Karen until I got an answer and then all of my emotions came out. Finally, I got her on the phone and just wanted to talk to my daughter to see if she was ok. She let me talk to her briefly, and then pulled the phone away from her just to tease me. She kept saying she'd moved on and that things would be different now and that what I had going on in court was not going anywhere now so I better save my money because I was gonna need it.

While she was going on and on I could hear some dudes voice in the background, so I started to call him out. *"Fuck that nigga you wit, he's a bitch to me! I hear him talking in the background; tell that bitch ass nigga to shut the fuck up!"*

By now, she has handed her new boyfriend the phone and all I could hear is her saying in the background *"Yeah he will whoop your ass nigga, yeah what you gonna do?"*

So I'm like *"who the fuck is this?"*

He started to talk and I told him to *"shut the fuck up!"*

He kept saying *"come see me, come see me, I'ma thug in the street!"*

I asked him his name and he said *"Mike"*
…and Mike where did you meet her?
"In the club."

I just started laughing hysterically and he kept trying to talk and I just keep laughing.
I told him that this had nothing to do with him at all. This was between me and her and my kids. He just kept talking and she was in the background talking shit like he was gonna do something to me.

I told him that plain and simple that if it came down to it "I would kill anyone who came in between me and my kids!" I was fired up, at that point, how dare she get some lame ass nigga to get on the phone with me and saying some off the wall shit *"I'ma thug in the streets!"* Come on man, you know that's some bamma ass shit. If you about it you don't say any corny shit like that and furthermore, it's just a code.

"Mind your own business," and this was none of his anyway. I was dealing with some true bammas! I was really lost now and was reckless and had crazy thoughts running through my head. I just zoned out and in the background I could just hear this dude trying to get my attention:

"James! James! James! James! James!"

My kids being around this guy; who swears up and down that, he's a thug, and their mother making dumb moves, I was at my wit's end. I hung up.

For the next week I could not concentrate on work or anything else. That conversation just kept playing over and over in my mind. It consumed me and I thought of all the worse possible scenarios, playing over in my head. The more I thought about it more hopeless I felt. When I could not take it anymore, I sat down and put pen to paper. It was about 11 pm. I addressed my letter to my mom, dad and my family. This was eating me up inside.

I just wanted so bad to react to the situation and make them pay. I was so used to going off the muscle, reaching out and touching somebody. But I couldn't. I had too much to lose, or did I?

Shit! I wasn't getting anywhere with the courts before and now I got to put up with this. I know that it's all talk but damn just the principle.

How this clown gonna challenge me? Tryna call me out? Ok you can be whatever you want to be on the phone, "thug in the streets," but when I see you . . . ughhh when I see you I'ma break your fucking jaw! And you!? How the fuck you gonna go there? Man I'ma smack the shit out of you!!!! My kids!!! Damn! Well fuck it! Don't seem like shit gonna workout in my favor so I might as well handle this shit and go hard! Yeah I'ma punish that motherfucka, fucking wit me? Fucking wit me? I got you Mike, you better start running cause I ain't stopping, and you fucked with the wrong nigga now . . . I'm done, I'm done, she got the audacity to put that nigga on the phone!!! Fuck this shit, it's over it's over. I might as well call it quits because I'd rather be dead than to have a motherfucka carry me and get away with it, especially with my kids man!!! Awww man!!!! I'ma kill'em!

I was seriously thinking about taking this dude out. He had threatened me and I felt that I had to react now. But I had to listen to reason right now, even though I wanted to just go and do something to them. I knew I had to just take time and think. I hadn't gotten anywhere just yet at court here in Georgia, hitting a brick wall, but was making slow progress.

I had to think.

That conversation kept playing over and over in my head that week. I got a phone call from my aunt, she was checking up on me.

"Hey little James, how are you doing?"

I told her what happened with the phone conversation and she just assured me *"Look, they tryna trip you up and make you do something and get you in trouble, just ignore them, she got issues all things will work out for you in time. I know you want to knock them upside the head..."*

We spoke for an hour and laughed and I felt a little better after that. Something weighed heavy on my mind and I just could not get it out. I thought about my kids and got scared for them. What if somebody did something to them, I'm not there to protect them. I'm battling with myself the Devil and God. Envisioning what happens at the end, just thinking . . .

I sat down again and started writing—a letter to my mother, father, brother and sister. And in it I started to explain to them how I felt . . .

"I'm sorry but I can't go on living like this

and just sitting by while God knows what is happening to my kids, this may be the last time that you hear from me… "

…and just then I stopped!

I thought about the next step, I set my alarm. I planned on getting me a drink then finish the letter and then bounce at 4am. I had just finished planning and nothing else was on my mind other than getting at them!

Shit, the courts were not gonna help me out. They were just gonna do whatever and have me stuck in this life of hell dealing with this woman. I sat at my computer and stared at the screen wondering, what else? I wanted so badly to just get up and go out and get that drink and finish what I started and prepare to ride out the next morning. I asked God, "What do you want me to do? What do I need to do? Help Me God!"

I sat at my computer and pulled up my web browser…sat there for a minute and something came over me and I typed in: Maryland.gov.

Wondering why I came to this site, I heard my lawyers voice in my head, *"Now remember she can go into any court and file for full custody and everything that you have done so far will be null and void."* I had told him in the beginning to never give me any bad news, he wanted to be politically correct and I sided with the thought of having hope. I browsed through the site and pulled up court cases and entered my name in the defendant column. The result came back 1549 matches!

Damn! I didn't realize that my name was that popular! This gonna take me forever to get through!

"Persistence pays off" echoed in my head I searched through the cases. I had searched the cases all night! I stopped to refocus my eyes and looked at the clock; it was now 3:58am! I focused my eyes back to the computer screen. Damn! I could not believe my eyes there was a case against me for domestic violence in Maryland.

Now I hadn't been in Maryland for almost a year and a half. How the hell was this possible? I looked over at the clock and it was 3:58. I shut the alarm off and looked over the information and noticed that I only had a day and a half to show up and give an answer to the court. I looked at the filing date, I had spoken to her earlier the day that she went to have it filed—February 28th at different times that day once around 9:44am and another time around 12:23pm.

I keep track of our conversations and all other types of communication, recorded or texted. I was headed to work and on a lunch break during the times I texted her and we spoke about the medicine that my daughter was taking. Around 3pm that day she went in and filed the domestic violence charges against me in Maryland. I found out about this court case on March 5th and I had to be in court on March 7th. I had been to my lawyer's office earlier that week, in Georgia, to finish up paperwork and to the clerk's office which included petition of contempt of a standing order, a child support worksheet, petitions for legitimating, with all other supportive documents. This was her way to stop the proceedings in Georgia with a court case of her own, and it outlined: Temporary, Court Orders: Shall not abuse, shall not contact shall not enter residence, shall stay away from school shall stay away from employment and custody. This order was affective from February 28th to March 7th and I could not contact her during that period and she was trying to trip me up.

I received a text message on March 2nd at 12:53am from her. Luckily, I did not answer that text cause then I would have been in violation of a temporary order through Maryland courts. Like my mom always say is that *"man plans a plan and God's plans, and he is truly the best of planners."*

I felt it was nothing short of God changing my mind that night to search the web instead of getting drunk and finishing that letter. I went to work the next day to tell my manager in person that I had to go to Maryland that night so I could answer to this case. I had no idea of how I was going to make it to Maryland; I had 62 dollars to my name. Driving from Atlanta to Maryland was not going to work; I could get only to Richmond before I ran out of gas. I expressed to my supervisor that I needed to go; company policy was that I could not miss any days under my first 90 new hire period, but I had no choice. A co-worker of mine overheard our conversation. She

said *"give me 60 dollars and I will get you a round trip ticket,"* as she jumped up from her seat. I prayed on it as I gave her the 60 dollars; please let this be real if not I'm gonna go to jail…Amen."
That day I got a call from another job I had applied for and they gave me my start date, March 10th. Wow! With everything going on around me it was hectic to say the least. I called my new employer to just give them a heads up about the case, since my first day on the job was my birthday, March 10th.

I called my lawyer and let him know what had happened and he explained that this was a strategic move. Basically, an emergency hearing as a domestic violence case would and could trump my case and put a stop to our progress. We would have to get through this first before we could continue our case, so he wished me good luck. I called my new employers and discussed all the possibilities, and was not sure of the outcome, but they assured me that they would be right there in my corner and would see me through.

The outcome or even the amount of time that this thing would go on was unknown and at this time I needed all the support that I could get. I hadn't even started work with them yet and they were already saying they had my back, so that was one less thing to worry about. I arrived at the airport and sure enough all of my information was there in the computer! Still in awe, how in the world? God answered all of my prayers in one day. I only had 60 dollars to my name and HE made it all possible, I boarded the plan now with 2 dollars to my name. I called my father and mother and let them know what was going on. My dad met me at the airport and dropped me off at mom's house.

The plan was that he would come back in the morning and we would both drive over to the courthouse to see what was going on. That night I talked to my mom about the charges that I was facing and she was confident that everything would turn out right. She knew that I was doing the right thing by my kids and that I did not do what they were trying to charge me with. She encouraged me to take control of the situation and do not let anyone have control over me. Stay calm and think before I say anything and just know that I would be victorious.

Three Ring Circus

My dad met me at my mom's house at 7 am and we headed to the courthouse. Neither of us knew what to expect because, just talking to the lawyer the day before, it could've possibly gone any direction. I was facing up to 10 years in prison, if they believed this lie.

Once we got to the courthouse I took a deep breath and looked at my Dad and said *"let's do this."*

We went first to the clerk's office to pick up the affidavit and see what in the world this thing is about. I give the clerk my Information and they acted puzzled. They don't know why I was there, so there was some confusion as to why I hadn't got a copy of the affidavit, I soon found out why.

Reading through the first part of the affidavit, they had the wrong address; better yet, she put down the wrong address. I called over the Sheriff and showed him my ID and told him that I would have never gotten served with this because they had the wrong address. He shook his head and wished me luck. *"Man they should throw this thing out, cause if you weren't even here in the state of Maryland when she said that all this happened then you good."*

I read further and couldn't believe what I was reading—naw I'm playing, I could believe it, and it was all a lie. Now my thing was, how in the world are they gonna prove what was written down on the affidavit when supposedly all of this happened in the state of Georgia but was being heard in Maryland.

I got the whole gist of what was going on. She figured she could go behind my back and pull this case out of the air to try and trump what was already in motion in Georgia. No coincidence that she would do this around the same time. Someone who knew a little about something, told her to do it to trump my case. The problem is that now that I showed up and found out about the case, she had no clue that I was there. What she was banking on as the Sheriff explained was "*if you did not show up and they could not get in touch with you through the mail, then the case would be heard and they would put a warrant out for your arrest, cause to them they gave you enough time and notification about this case for you to answer to it, too bad if it had went to the wrong address that's the one they had on file for you, and basically you would have been locked up.*"

All of this was now sinking in and I was ready to get this thing done and over with. I could not wait to see the look on her face when she saw me in that courtroom.

Sitting outside waiting for them to open the doors, a lot of things ran through my mind. I thought about what I would say once I saw her, what I was going to tell the judge. I had prepared for this type of thing for the last year. I had gathered and saved just about everything, and I made a point to CYA—Cover My Ass!

I'd recorded everything; keep records, phone, bills, letters, dates, and times. I had done my homework and when it came to the law; pertaining to my legitimating case and even this one, I was ready. The night that I found out about the case I started putting together my game plan, reading through any and all related cases that I could find all things relative to my specifics, Maryland law... all of it.

I had the same feeling of anxiousness that I felt when I was younger, at a football game first kickoff, wrestling match anticipating the whistle, the beginning of a fight. This was far from fear that most people associate with anxiety, but a thirst and happiness I felt, knowing that I was about to get into it and whoop your monkey ass!

I loved the feeling of showing my opponent up, whoever you are, I loved the battle, I'm a soldier and I was at war! The doors opened and no sign of Karen. Good for me anyway, I still had the element of surprise. I remember growing up and being blamed for something that I didn't do, but had no way to prove that I didn't do it and that stayed with me, I hated to be blamed for something I didn't do and I made it a point later on in life to face my accusers. I'ma make you tell it to my face and deal with you. So, bring it! We sat in the back of the courtroom waiting for her arrival and getting this three-ring circus going. The judge came in and the proceedings were called to order, and still no sign of Karen, then in walks her father. He was looking around for a place for them to sit, he turned over his left shoulder and there I was starring him in the eyes.

Man, I wish I had a damn camera right then and there to take that picture; he acts like he saw a damn ghost! Karen walked in behind him, looked back and saw me sitting there and literally wanted to shit on herself.

She ran up to the judge's bench yelling *"I want a continuance!"* She interrupted what the judge was doing so he stopped and wanted to hear from me what was going on as he did his role call. I looked at my dad; he was in the back with his sunglasses on, yeah too damn gangsta! My man, he just gave me a slight smirk.

The judge asked me how was I doing this morning, and I answered "not too well being that I had to come up here to answer to this lie." He asked me where I'd come from and I told him from Georgia, and he replied *"Wow, well we will try and get done and over with to get you back home, ok?"*

This was all new to him also, he took his time to read over the affidavit then he stopped and asked me had I been served. I told him I got the affidavit this morning from the clerk's office and he said well you haven't officially been served yet, so he summoned the Sheriff to come out and serve me formally. Surprise. It was the same Sheriff that I spoke to earlier that morning. He came over to me and said *"Man I already served you this morning, what they doing?"*

He turned to the judge and was interrupted, and he turned back to me and said, *"This some bullshit man, good luck."* So now I was officially served and we could go on with the proceedings.

This is it. Time to put up or shut up, I was brought all the way out here for this bullshit and now it was time for war. The judge took a long pause and with his head down he flipped through the pages. Ok now, Mr. Simms what would you like to do, either take a continuance on this case or shall we proceed.

"No continuance, I want to do this right now!"

"This is my understanding, this case is about domestic violence that occurred or not occurred in the state of Maryland or Georgia? I'm not really clear... Mr. Simms how did you find out about this court date, if you were not served?"

"I found out on the internet! If you look at the affidavit, it has the wrong address on it."

"What say you on this matter?" as he nodded his head towards Karen and looked back down, flipping through the pages again.

Karen just looked at the judge, trying to process the judge's question, and then looked at me with disgust. I guess she had to try to remember exactly what she herself had written down, and it seemed to be escaping her.

She got herself together and told the judge that it had all happened in both states. Right then and there the judge stopped everything...

"Hold on, wait, wait . . . this is all confusing...Mr. Simms do you have legal counsel? Yes, ok and M'am, do you have counsel?"

"No, I don't. But I did meet with the House of Ruth, but . . ." Karen was cut off by the judge.

"I advise that you go and secure counsel, and I will proceed with the next case. We will continue ... call the next case..."

Wow. To me it just seemed a little unfair, because I didn't even start this case but I came prepared and she didn't I think they should just throw this thing out. I looked over a Karen and her face said it all. Her eyes were now bloodshot red, teary and she kept shaking. I looked back over my shoulder and shrugged my shoulders at my dad, it was not over yet. It took about almost two hours before Karen and her legal counsel came back to the courtroom.

The judge heard both sides and shared the same point that I was making, *"This court has no jurisdiction in this case if in fact all of the alleged abuse happened in the state of Georgia."*

He was about to make his ruling when Karen's legal counsel asks could she approach the bench. She whispered something to the judge and he nodded. *"Well due to the other parties involved in this case, I am compelled to have this case continued and the court orders the Department of Social Services to conduct an investigation and report back to the court."*

Now, I had already been in touch with the Department of Social Services from the day that Karen had taken Mya away and I called on a daily basis to assure that they would investigate her for her actions. The judgment would now force them do an investigation, because even my numerous calls seemed to have no effect on the caseworker. My main concern was the safety and well-being of my kids, since Karen was not thinking rationally. My lawyer explained to me that the investigation would clear me of everything so I would just have to be patient.

So, disappointed I left the courthouse, I was back home so it was time to mingle and get a little stress out. I called my brother and I got back in touch with one of my sisters. I did not have a rental car so he picked me up and dropped me off at her house. She wanted to see me and we would hang out that night before I went back home and she would take me to my mom's house the next day. I spent the day with my sister and her friends. I called a couple of my old friends just to catch up and let them know that I was back in town. I had to make sure that, in an event that something happened; I had a backup plan and someone looking out for me. The visit was a short one, because I had to catch a flight the next morning, and everything was set in place so I headed home.

Staying The Course

I had a lot to do when I got back to Georgia. Once on the flight, I started rebuilding my case—from the point where I'd found out about the case to all the phone calls, text messages, dates times and pictures. I went to see my lawyer and give him proof of the court case in Maryland. He advised me that we just had to wait and see how this case was going to end. He said from his experience that this type of case could trump the case that we had going in Georgia, whenever an emergency case comes up.

Now my paperwork in Georgia was on hold because of the trial in Maryland, but at least it was complete. My mind and all of my energy was set on putting my case together, since she was alleging child abuse and abuse to her and the other kids I had to have proof. Compiling all of the evidence would be simple. I was determined to prove my case so I started researching like cases.

Even though my lawyer made me aware of the possibility that things could go the other way I was still determined to fight even harder and prepare and do all that I could to defend myself. First I started with the domestic violence charge, what it meant and more importantly the definition of it under Maryland law. I knew that in order to have a fair chance, I had to get in tune with the law. I pulled up information on Maryland Domestic Violence Laws, studied them.

I researched the outcome of about 40 different cases, some where there was proof of domestic violence and others that it was alleged and from there I started creating my foundation of my case. Re-reading over the affidavit, I noticed things that jumped out at me that I could use to build my case. Charged with domestic violence against my kid's mother, my daughter, son and step daughter, but the abuse of my daughter and kids mother was spelled out more.

She alleged that I beat my daughter, covering her mouth and telling her that her mother does not love her and since she had moved on, those threats had been made stating that I knew where she stayed. She alleged that I made threats to come to her house and kill her and anyone coming between my kids. This was not a coincidence, the week that she came and took my daughter, I called CPS and they scheduled a home visit to her aunt's house to see how the kids were doing. So I marked that down as her statement of how I knew where she stayed--and just so happened she went and filed this petition the day after CPS visited her and the kids.

The other information stated that threats of violence, mental injury of a child, and stalking were involved, all in the state of Georgia. I went through the Temporary Protective Order with a fine tooth comb, to find any other holes in her testimony that I would argue in court. During my research of court cases and the process of law, I learned that in the State of Maryland, when domestic violence is filed, that the Petitioner (which was her), is required to prove the alleged facts by "clear and convincing evidence" The law also mentioned that this would be difficult to do if you do not have law training, so they suggest hiring a lawyer. In other words, she would have to prove the cause without a shadow of a doubt. But I was not going to rely on her to prove her point, so I continued to gather my evidence.

I noticed that there were errors on the petition, which I had become familiar with in my quest to finish my paperwork in Georgia, attention to detail and clear language could only be approved by the court. In the line asking the address of the abuser she filled in the wrong address for me, and also added the same address on the line of "At this time the victim can be found at" which clearly stated I was the alleged abuser and victim at the time the petition was filed.

Like I said, with my history of filing court papers I knew that the smallest thing as grammatical errors would deem your petition incomplete by the court and you would have to resubmit the petition. I also outlined other key facts to this case, the alleged bruise that my daughter had on her hand, which she had as a result of her breakout back in October. I documented them back then with pictures and now they would answer these allegations. I kept track of dates. I gathered together all receipts, school records, doctors, dermatologist reports, timecards from work, notes from coworkers, friends, babysitter and a police report for that week to establish my whereabouts and events.

I pressed on with my case building, and I looked on the web. I pulled up domestic violence attorneys back when I found out about this case and put in my comments in the search section. I received an immediate response back to my questions.

Now I did not know who it was that responded back to me but he was straight to the point and I decided that he would be my lawyer. Kind of a crazy way to pick a lawyer right? But I had my whole case laid out, so I figured that a lawyer with some sense would do, he just had to show up and be my mouthpiece. Judges seem to just ignore you if you do not have legal counsel, it seems so now I had a lawyer and a good friend of mine helped me with the payment to secure counsel.

That whole two weeks I was anxious to get to court and prove my case, I couldn't think about anything else. It was my first week on the new job and I was making a list of things that needed to be done and just trying to settle down into my role and learn the ropes. The legal process was now becoming second nature to me, the ups and downs, and there were no shortages of new surprises around every corner.

Surprise, Surprise, Surprise

I took off from work that week. I would have to drive back to Maryland for this court case. I arrived at my lawyer's office a day earlier than expected.

I had the money sent via FedEx to speed up the process, and secure him as my attorney of record. As I sat in his office I had no clue—as in, never met him, just talked to him over the phone and by text messages. But from all of our communication he seemed like a good lawyer.

His office was in a highly populated Hispanic part of town and I could tell that along with the numerous other types of cases that he took on, that the bulk of his work dealt with Hispanics and a lot of domestic violence cases. From what I could tell, he had what I thought was either a Jewish or Irish last name. The stereotype around the way was that if you came to court with a white lawyer—Jewish or not you had a better chance to win.

Hey I don't make the stereotypes up I just hear them.

In this case I didn't care what ethnicity he was, just as long as he could represent me in the fairest way, hear me out and work with the case that I had laid out.

I waited for him for close to two hours. I

was there early, right when his offices opened their doors. I knew that he was a busy man so I wanted to get all of the particulars out the way, give him time to go over our plan and get on with his day so we could be ready for court in the next day or so.

He finally arrived and we spoke briefly about the case, but his mind was on collecting his fee, before we went any further. I didn't blame him. The FedEx had not gotten there yet and I was anxious. I had all the copies of the check and all for him but he still needed cash in hand. We went ahead and talked about the case, because he was confident that the money would be in by close of business that day, plus by that point we had built a good rapport.

I expressed all of my concerns and showed him that I was serious and that I had compiled all the necessary information that he would need to prove my case. I also gave him my other lawyer's information back in Georgia and built a time line for him about all the events that lead up to this point. We concluded the meeting, and he said that he would call me when the money had gotten in, so I left and went back to my mom's house, picked up lunch and went to sleep. I was exhausted, and I drove from Georgia to Maryland almost nonstop.

The lawyer called me later on that day and confirmed that everything was a go and I prepared for the next day to battle it out in court. By this point, I had already collected all the information that I had needed in the Georgia case for legitimating, but now I needed much more. I had to prove to the court that without a reasonable doubt that I did not commit this crime and was going to have to be prepared to have all the info front and center for the court.

I headed out to court and I was ready now to have my say and for my lawyer to go to battle for me. I got to the parking garage early. I parked and made my way to the courthouse. I was early so I had to wait nervously outside. The doors to the courthouse opened at 8 and I still had minutes to spare since we weren't scheduled to appear until 8:45.

This time I was appearing in court with just myself and my lawyer—my father was going to join us later. I had called ahead of time to my folks and let them know about me going to court, just in case we had some type of drama during the time that I was back; I had folks looking out for me. I watched every minute of the clock outside of the courthouse door, and I spotted an old associate from an old neighborhood I lived in years ago.

He was up there for traffic court and I just filled him in on all the drama going on in my life. We went back on some things that had happened back in the day and he assured me that things were gonna be alright. He told me he had just had a new baby girl and I congratulated him on his new addition to his family. He told me was getting married sometime the next summer. He had left his past alone and was turning over a new leaf and this was just a little hiccup, a traffic ticket but all and all everything was cool. He was good peoples and it was good to see somebody that I knew out there. I was a bit paranoid and excited at the same time, just wondering what was in store for me today.

I took time to say a prayer and think back to all the things that my mother, aunts, family members and friends had said to me to keep me encouraged and focused and it made me smile. I went through the metal detectors and had my briefcase checked, this briefcase would be my lifeline and carrier of all important information. It held my key to freedom, and security, it was my world, right there in my hand. It's a red and black briefcase with a three ring binder, a section with pocket separators a zippered pouch and a netted sleeve a "Case it" briefcase. It was my mobile office and war room all my ammunition was placed there and shows up with me every time I'm in court.

I made my way into the courthouse and up the stairs to wait outside of the courtroom until they opened up. My lawyer showed up and we spoke about the case and he asked me *"has anyone showed up yet?"*

"Naw not yet," I responded. Ten minutes later, here comes my kid's mom with some skinny dude.

She refused to make eye contact but gestured to him that I was sitting there. *"Is that the thug in the streets?"* my lawyer asked, as we both smirked.

Picture a skinny dude attempting a mean mug, nothing menacing at all, real funny to me. We walked into the courtroom behind them and took our seats. Skinny dude kept looking my way and trying to give me the pseudo mean mug, and all I could do was laugh, and just think how much I wanted to just reach out and touch this dude and break his jaw. It's just something that is not done and let go—someone staring you down without you tapping that chin. We were in court so I couldn't do anything but just look back. I remember thinking to myself, *"Really? This dude? This is who you got going up against me? Damn clown, ohh man I'ma knock him out."*

So my lawyer and I are going over our case and I'm just trying to keep my cool because dude is just staring at me. I *really* want to just jump over there and break his jaw. I see him talking to my kid's mother and making gestures like he was questioning her. At one point I was reading his lips and I could have sworn he said *"so what you want me to do, if I kill'em then what?"*

I asked my lawyer if the courtroom was fully mic'd?

"Yeah, why?"

I told him that dude was loud enough to have been heard saying what I thought he said. My lawyer went back and asked to hear the playback, but they could not make out what was said. We waited for our time to be in front of the judge and we just watched my kid's mother and her lawyers get their act together.

She had hired The House of Ruth, a women's lawyer defense group for female victims of domestic violence. I spoke with my lawyer and he gave me the rundown on what was going to happen. We spoke about the judge ordering an investigation and how an investigation, even though it would take some time, would be in my best interest so it would clear me of all of these charges.

"Don't worry; we still need to prove your innocence and this is how the process will go, more than likely they will continue this case."

Hell naw! What do you mean? Continue this case!? I ain't got the time to keep coming back up here. I just started my new job and can't be missing all these days!

My lawyer leaned in closer and said. *"Unfortunately, this is the only way to do it, plus they will order an investigation, they have to prove what they are alleging."* Ok if that's what it was going to take to clear myself of these charges, I was ready.

Karen and her lawyers left the room, I guess to sit down and plan their case right then and there, but we were confident and waiting. When it was our time, I asked my lawyer if I could do something. He asked what. I said I wanted to give her lawyers a copy of my evidence.

"Why?"

Because I had nothing to lose and I knew that whatever they were planning, I could turn her lawyers against her. They have to look at the facts and not hearsay. I figured this was the best tactic because it would show them up and put holes through their case. My lawyer advised me to hold that thought until later.

We had a new judge this time around so he had to get brought up to speed about the case and where we were pertaining to an investigation that was spelled out by the previous judge. It began and now I could be heard and argue my case.

Their first line of attack was putting her on the stand. The judge opened up on what was alleged in the petition and some catch up on how we got here. Her lawyers tried to paint a picture of a suffering woman who was scared and whose kids were abused and mistreated. She also added some drama to it by crying and just throwing out unfounded stories of abuse to her and my daughter.

When her lawyer asked her, *"What has Mr. Simms done to you that makes you feel threatened and asking the court for the TPO? (Temporary Protective Order)?"* She said, *"He makes threatening gestures towards me."*

Huh?

How could I make threatening gestures towards her? I was in Georgia!

Well back to the case and what it all detailed, allegedly I abused my kids and the mother of my kids in Georgia—the first week of

February, and now we are in court in Maryland for this alleged act. To try and keep you with me, I had physical custody of my daughter for six months up until the second week of February. Her mother was nowhere to be seen, makes no damn sense.

She explained to her lawyer and the judge that my daughter had marks on her hands and face, product of her being abused by me her father who she left in my custody for the last six months. My lawyer did not cross examine her, so they let her down off of the stand. She was upset and she looked my way with a look as to say "Now you in trouble." This one was for the books and had to be one of the biggest no no's in the world.

They called up their star witness and my lawyer and I really wanted to laugh, say it ain't so, it's "The thug in the streets"! Last time that I checked thugs won't get caught dead in a courtroom in the plaintiff's corner, let alone get on the stand! Where I'm from that's called "snitching" and snitches get stitches!

They call him, the new boyfriend to the stand and now he is in the hot seat and doesn't look all tough and confident anymore. They ask him to give his name and address. "I'm my name is Andre Roubenson and my address is 5302 Englewood Dr in Hyattsville, MD…" right then my lawyer jumped up.

"*Hold on, could you speak a little louder and repeat that for me?*" Karen's lawyers objected and wanted to know why.

"Well this man threatened my client and we need to know who he is." I whispered to my lawyer, *"I thought his name was Mike"*

Now this really rattled dude because he started shaking from that point on. If he was such a thug, why was he shaking? He acted like it was cold in the courtroom. Everything that he had said over the phone had just caught up with him right at that moment and it was too much for him to deal with. I stared at him and smiled. Now it was really on, and it was too late for him. Just him getting on that stand put him out there, and even giving up fake addresses was not gonna get him out of the hot seat either. That was a slick move.

I guess they discussed that part when they were in the back planning their case and I couldn't stop myself from wanting to laugh, because it was pitiful. Now he was giving his testimony and I kept staring at him, right through him and he got more and more nervous.

They asked him *"what relationship do you have with Mr. Simms?* And he answered, *"none."* He said that he knew that I was the father of her kids and that was it. They wanted to show somehow that I had threatened to harm him and her personally so they asked him about the night we had first spoke and the nature of the conversation. He added that *"he said that he would kill anyone that came in-between him and his kids."* Before my lawyer could cross, the judge butted in and explained why that statement was not a threat. *"That is not a threat..."*

You should have been there! To see their faces, Karen, her lawyers and Mr. Super Thug on the stand, look like they lost their best friend. They were really banking on his testimony to be damaging to my case and some kind of eye opener. But it bounced back in their faces and you could just see the fear.

At this point, Super Thug started shaking uncontrollably, as the judge explained himself. *"It is not a threat because it was not a direct threat; he did not say your name directly, and anyone could be me, you, her or him. So it is not threat."* That shutdown plan B, now on to plan C. Her lawyers wanted desperately to prove that I was a threat and an abuser of Karen and my kids. So it was my turn to take the stand.

I was poised, not at all nervous. I had come prepared and was ready to fight this war head on. They called me to take the stand and I walked up, all the while just thinking through what was going to be asked and what my reaction to it was going to be. Whatever it was, I had to be cool as ice. I did a pre trial prayer before entering the courtroom and now was in a mode of prayer as I approached the stand. I asked God to strengthen me and keep me focus on the matter at hand and not to lose my temper.

The officer directed me to the stand and to stay standing while the judge asked me my name, address and raise my right hand to swear me in.

Her lawyer began. They wanted to use old text messages between me and Karen to establish a violent character. They mentioned that I was mad that Karen had left and that I was doing everything in my power to intimidate and harass her, so they started with the text messages. Her lawyer handed me her phone and asked me to read out loud the contents of the text message that she scrolled down to and pointed for me to read. I remembered sending the text message it was right around the time that she left and that Mya had gotten sick, I called her and got no answer then I texted her and she just responded that she had moved on and didn't care if I had a bun or not, but that she really didn't care to hear what I had to say. I was calling her because our daughter, her daughter had gotten sick and she needed her at that time to talk to her. My daughter was calling for her in her moment of pain and misery and she was not there and did not choose to even talk to her, she was done with us.

Now, the text that they had me to read was part of the conversation that we had that night. I'd been mad at her for saying the things that she said. When I questioned her how could she just up and leave her daughter and not even want to have any communication with her. I'd told her that Mya was feeling left out and really felt that she did not want her. Our conversation had gotten heated after a while and I finally got her on the phone to talk and she blurted out some shit that really took me over the top.

She said, in response to me telling her that our daughter was upset with her, *"Well maybe I should just treat this like another adoption and just say fuck her"*

My response was *"How the hell could you say that about your daughter? How can you put anyone before your daughter or even say some shit like that about her? You don't have to worry about her anymore since you just gonna just throw her away like that like you don't even love her and that's why she feels that way she does, because you just don't love her the same."*

She just kept on saying that she had moved on and had a life now and she has support so she didn't need us.

Her lawyer had me to read to the courtroom my response to what she had said last, because they wanted to show that it was all about her moving on and that I was mad that she moved on, and they failed to mention what the real issue was about my daughter. So I read the text out loud, I was basically telling her what I felt about her statement.

I mentioned that she was not a fit mother, and questioned how could she go and make some man more important than her own sick daughter. I started reading the text and then, I stopped. This text had nothing to do with the time line on this case. The texts were from 2007 and from a conversation I was having about the health of our daughter. The case was alleging domestic violence on her and the kids in February of 2008. I stopped right there, and told the judge that I had to explain what I was saying in that text message and give the background and time line.

"Your honor, this text was from 2007 when I called her to tell her that our daughter was sick, she had left her with me and took our other two kids with her. Plus it had no relevance to this case." Her lawyer jumped up.

"It is relevant to the case. This shows Mr. Simms' aggressive and violent nature."

I interjected, *"The text that I read did not have a date on it and I can prove that it is an old text."* I gestured to the judge. May I? And he nodded.

"How many text messages do you have?" I asked. Her lawyer answered, *"About 24 of them."*

I explained that during the alleged time there were over 60 text messages between the both of us and I had copies of every one of them and they were all dated. At that point I nodded to my lawyer to hand over the stack of texts.

I can prove that those were old text messages that had nothing to do with this current case or timeline. My lawyer got up after they decided they had no further questions and began to question me further. Suddenly, the judge interrupted him and said that the text messages would be thrown out. Another victory!

The judge told me that I could get off the stand and go back to my seat. They got shutdown again, and it felt great.

I had done my homework and it was definitely paying off. It was like I had a copy of their playbook. I made my way off the stand back to my seat with my head held high. I looked to the back of the courtroom at my Dad and he smiled— his seal of approval. I looked to my right as I took my seat and just watched as Karen's lawyers scrambled to see what else they could come up with. Karen's eyes were bloodshot red and she and the super thug both seemed to be very uneasy. They couldn't do anything but hang their heads.

This was not a game to me; it was a serious situation and I came prepared. Her lawyers couldn't think of anything else so they declined anymore testimony. Now justice would finally be served. We would get done with this three ring circus and I could get back to Georgia to work and finish off the process of being able to care for my children. As the judge started to make the ruling, we found out that the investigation had never been done.

I turned to my lawyer and just shook my head and he reiterated what he said before—that the investigation would clear me fully. And yeah, it was going to be a hassle to take more time out of my schedule to come back, but it would be all worth it in the end. I was somewhat disappointed that this thing did not end that day. I had won all the battles, but the war was not over. This time around I had driven up to Maryland and now had to make the long trip back to Georgia, tired mentally and with emotions running high I drove back home.

When I arrived back home, the first person that I paid a visit was my other lawyer, followed by my employer to let him know that I had to go back to court again.

Once at my lawyer's office, we discussed what was going on and all of the possibilities. He mentioned that Maryland could override anything that we had going on down here in case of an emergency hearing and could trump any decision that Georgia had made up until that point concerning legitimating my kids. He wanted me to look at the situation and the worst case scenario.

"If convicted of this there are several things that can happen; you will lose the opportunity to shared custody, visitation, and possible jail time, but we are looking into at least some kind of joint custody or visitation…"

I was not pleased at all with any of the options and definitely I wasn't trying to see jail. Now my fate was in the hands of Child Protective Services and my first plan of action was to give them a call and check the progress of the investigation. I had contacted them earlier at the beginning of all of this when Karen taken Mya from school. I called again and inquired about the case and who would be handling it. Not surprisingly, CPS had not heard about the investigation being ordered by either judge—the first or the last one.

I made it a point to stay fresh in their minds, so I would regularly call and fax letters to my contact at CPS. When I got in contact with Child Protective Services in Maryland they acted like it just wasn't that big of a deal to them to do the job of investigating this case. I called until I got a hold of my contact's supervisor because at that point, I was frustrated. If this thing went south, it would be the end of me. I wanted to show them that I was involved in my children's' lives and cared about them. I was also thinking how this could affect our lives and just erase my case and take away what I worked so hard for and years.

I kept calling and finally got what I was looking for—they had received the judge's orders and now we were going to proceed in their investigation. The order also had provisions for DFACS to do an investigation since they had somehow dropped the ball.

I called around until I got in contact with the Georgia CPS and left a message for the person who was responsible for their part of the investigation. I figured that my interest alone in this matter would prompt them to do the investigation without a certain bias. I just felt that in a case like this that naturally, it would be human nature to feel that the man did some kind of wrong. I was in that way of thinking because nine times out of ten it happens that way, and who wouldn't believe a woman's side of it. I had all of this stacked against me, not to mention that I was a young black male and statistically we are charged and convicted more often with certain crimes related to domestic violence. I had to put a human face on the investigation and planned to show them the other side of it and the real reason behind this bogus case. I put myself on front street for all to see and get to know, with all the facts of the case, ready for anyone who cared to listen. I got confirmation from both agencies and I would just have to wait until the investigation was done. I prayed more than I ever prayed before, *"God you got me this far, please don't drop me off, I need your help."*

Somebody Prayed for Me

From the beginning of my ordeal I was constantly reaching out to God for guidance, I knew that I had to think before I said or did anything. Along the way, I had a great reminder to stay still, my mom and aunt and close friends ministered to me during my time of struggle. I remember talking to my mom the day that Karen came and took Mya away. I was in a heavy emotional state. All I could do was see red and worry about the well being of my daughter.

"What happened?" asked my mom.

"Well, I was at work and the babysitter called me and told me that Mya never got off the bus. I told her to go back to the school to go and pick her up...maybe she missed the bus. I got the call back from the babysitter, she wasn't there either and no one can tell me where she was. At that time my heart dropped, I could not breathe, this is my child and she was nowhere to be found..."

I went over that day with my mom and expressed my anger and my concern for my child's well-being, it had been six months since the last time that her mother had spoken to her or even seen her, and just out of the blue she shows up and takes her!

We spoke about that day and also touched on what had happen six months ago. She noticed that my faith was being tested to the utmost and she asked, *"Where is God in your life? Whenever you are going through something that you cannot handle look to him and he will aide you in your endeavors. What you need to do is read Job. It is the shortest book in the Bible and once you are done with it and understand it all of this will be over."*

That night I opened my Bible and took a look at Job, scrolling through it I said to myself, "the shortest book in the Bible? Wow mom set me up…" It was longer than what she said. But I read anyway, and started my journey of gaining my faith back again. I started reading Job the very minute that we got off the phone. I noticed that Job was being tried in a tremendous way, and I felt that I was too. I would normally react in one way and that was to fight or try to stop others bad habits, if you talked too much then you needed to get your mouth busted! Yeah I had a long way to go, and it was not gonna be an easy process without out a constant reminder and divine intervention. My mom, with her wisdom, set me on a path to self discovery and a deeper connection with even greater attributes of God, patience and faith.

I stayed on track everyday reading Job and taking it all in on how much he had to endure and amazingly he stands still and faithful in God even though when he was tested with the loss of his love ones and even his own life's comforts and possessions. I had reached a point that now I needed financial help. I was facing another trial and how would I act now?

God was stripping me of everything at this moment, my health, wealth, mind set, and attitude. I was being worked on and I became humbler each day. I noticed that his grace was there all around me. Yeah, I had lost faith, and I thought I had it all under control. I learned from reading Job, the process of God testing your faith to him, is that he would present you with things of great weight, hunger, fear, loss of material things, loss of life or limb, and test your will to stay sane. I was going through it all, it seems like money just would not either come to me or it was fleeting away from me fast in so many different forms. I had made money and material things bigger objects of praise and worth than God. So I was stripped of it all, and left to his mercy and will and it would be his will that would sustain me.

I was blessed with good friends in my life to be there to help and aide me in my process and I am forever grateful for God bringing them into my life. God worked on my mindset. I was always too proud to ask anyone for help, I did just about everything on my own in life cause I just felt that I could not leave anything for chance when I allowed someone else to do it for me. It was even my pride that would have stopped me from receiving Gods gifts for me in my time of need, but

I learned how to deal with my pride and humble myself. God humbled me.

I always knew that prayer and faith in the higher power would get you through tough times, but every now and then during my ordeal, I questioned my faith. I needed to be shown in order for me to just let go and believe. I struggled many nights against Gods will and my own, asking why He would do this, why He would do that.

I continued to read. I also got encouragement from other family members who helped me in my infant stages of gaining a strong faith in Gods ability to take control and move my situation in my favor. My aunt started calling me on a regular basis right about a month into the ordeal. She would be like "Lil James how are you doing today?" I loved the conversations that we had. It had been a long time since we had actually had a deep conversation, let alone as an adult. It did a lot for me during that time. I was building my spiritual base, learning patience and building a stronger bond with family. We would talk and just laugh about life; she would tell me not to even worry about the kids, because God would not let anything happen to them.

I heard her, but still I worried about what was going on and what was happening? She helped me put it all into perspective. *"You are doing what you are supposed to do for your family, God sees that and he will remember that. Boy don't even worry about her, all dogs have their day, so you will see just hang on it there."*

Each time that I got weak, I would go back
to what my aunt said, what my mom had me read,
the care that my friends showed me, by the grace
of God and reenergize because I knew that it was
not over. I was being prayed for now twenty-four
seven and I was deeper into my faith, so as I went
to court and dealt with my accusers, and laid down
my burdens I became stronger and I grew up.

I was just about done with reading Job and
getting a greater understanding of his faith and
mine, the investigations had comeback and I was
found not guilty! I had success!

My mom was right, my aunt was right! I
did prevail, and I was completely sound in the faith
that God would take care of my situation. I had just
gotten back to Georgia after the decision and that
week I had to make up some work, so I went in on
a Saturday. I had developed calm over my body,
mind and soul. I was untouchable, nothing could
get to me to shake my faith anymore because it had
been shown to me, and God had my back!

I was working changing filters at work on
the fourth floor, taking down ceiling tiles and
getting a filter count and checking the units
operations when I got a call. It was my mom's
friend and my mom was on the other line.

All I could hear was her crying in the back
ground. My heart dropped, I did not know what
was going on...she slowly told me.

"There was an accident and your aunt

Connie did not make it and they are not sure if your cousin is gonna make it... the kids were in the car..."

I jumped off the ladder and everything went completely deaf. I could hear my mom crying and her friend talking but I was in another world. I had just talked to Connie that week—about the trial and how good God is. We talked about my cousin; she told me how proud she was with his new found love for life and his career goals once he got out of jail. She encouraged me to raise above all the pettiness and put on the armor of God and go to war!

I cried there on the floor at work, my situation was no situation anymore. I prayed to God and asked him for an explanation, why? God Why? I cried and just lay on the floor. All the things that we talked about came back to me in a flash, *"Stay focused, God will take care of you and your kids, Lil James you are doing a good job, don't let them make you do something you will regret, don't buy those wolf tickets!"*

I had come all this way and I learned how to hold my tongue and take full responsibility for my actions and thoughts and I had her to thank for it all. I couldn't now lose my way, my mom, my aunt and I know grandma prayed for me. I stayed focus with their words echoing in my mind. I stood up and began to celebrate her life, remembering all the good times. They gave me strength in the time that I was losing it and came through in the nick of time. My aunt was laid to rest. I kept my promise to her to let God take control of the situation and everything will be alright! Somebody prayed for me during my darkest hour.

Sweet Justice

What I was facing was losing the chance to see my kids and time away somewhere in the neighborhood of up to ten years in jail, losing my license in the trade I spent 4 years in school for, and having something on my record so ugly and shameful that would ruin my life.

Now was the waiting game and I could not concentrate on anything, not at work, couldn't eat or sleep. I was stressed. The judge had ordered us to come back to the court after the processing of the investigation, which did not take that long at all. I came home and saw that a brochure was tacked to my door. It read "A Parents' Guide to a Child Protective Services (CPS) Investigation," and there was a name and number on the back of it and in the notes column it said "Please Call Me."

I went inside and called. I asked to speak with the case manager and she recognized my voice right away. She told me that the investigation was complete, in both Georgia and Maryland and this time both states took the time to investigate thoroughly. She told me that they interviewed all of the kids, and that not one of them spoke of any abuse from me to them, and that the investigation had cleared me of any of the alleged charges.

I could hear it in her voice that she felt what I felt, and was relieved that it was over. She congratulated me for sticking in there and taking care of my kids and stepping up, when so many other men didn't. Then she gave me a heads up to what to expect when I made it back to Maryland for the next court appearance. At that moment, the weight of the world was lifted off of my shoulders. I called my family and friends to let them know the good news. They were excited for me, and relieved that this did not have to go any further. I packed some clothes and put them in my car took a shower and set my alarm clock. I slept for 4 hours and then it was time to hit the road.

I arrived early that morning. The case time was supposed to begin at 1:15, so I had plenty of time to spare. I went to a friend's house and got some sleep. When I woke up it was still kind of early and I had about 3 more hours until I had to show up. I thought about the next step in this whole process. I had had also found out I'd been given a May 7th court date in Georgia for legitimating so I was happy about that—finally.

I got up and drove the rest of the way to the courthouse. When I got there, I called my lawyer. He had no idea of the good news. "*The investigation is over and I just found out that they cleared me of everything, my kids spoke up for me, so it's over.*"

I thanked him and told him I would see him when he got there. I called a couple of my friends and let them know that I was back in town and at the courthouse and gave them the rundown. My father said that he would come later on to see how I was doing. Hopefully they would grant me a chance to at least see the kids. I was waiting in the courtroom when the doors opened, sitting there just in anticipation to see the look on their faces when the judge read the verdict.

After a while the court room started to fill and Karen and her man were nowhere to be found. The court clerk started the roll call. Shortly after the announcement of our case, Karen and her lawyers came into the court room. The cases that preceded us were minor—a father not bringing the son home on time, a woman wanting more child support from the man who was already over paying to please her. The court room circus went on for about an hour past the limit. We weren't heard until about 2:30. It was our time to hear the verdict. I was excited to actually hear the words come from the judge's mouth that I was not guilty of any crime against my kids or her.

As the judge read over the information that he received from the clerk there was dead silence. I looked over at Karen and her man sitting there. This time there was no mean mugging or any type of gestures. They were quiet. Maybe they knew the verdict already. I turned around and as the judge started on our case. He told me to stand up.

The judge started, clearing his throat, *"upon examining the evidence of this case and the investigation performed by CPS, the court finds that there was no clear and convincing evidence*

on the petitioner's part to show that the respondent
committed an act of abuse against the respondent
or said children, this case is dismissed."

Those words echoed in my mind for a minute. I shook my lawyer's hand then looked over to my right. Karen and her boyfriend and lawyers were heading out the courtroom door. I asked the judge *"Well what about me seeing my kids?"*

He said *"Well you can go see your kids, the circuit court has determined jurisdiction."*

Ok, I said. I turned to my lawyer and asked him what that meant. He said that we would have to make some kind of arrangement with her. I knew that would be a hard sell to get her to let me see my kids, but it was worth a shot. My lawyer and I left the court room in search of Karen and her lawyers. They hadn't left the courthouse so we went to the House of Ruth offices. I looked through a glass window of one of the first doors and didn't see anyone. We went down the hall and I looked into a second window, and there they were just the door separating us.

I knocked on the window while staring at them; now talk all that shit dude! As I thought, looking dead into my accusers faces. I opened the door and my lawyer came in right behind me. I didn't really want to talk, just fight. He pulled me back as he noticed that I was getting closer. They didn't say anything—could not even look me in the face. My lawyer said that he would talk to them and told me to take a step outside and wait until he had negotiated some kind of deal with them.

So I waited for about 10 minutes. I watched the clock and man it felt like an hour. Finally my lawyer came out of the room with a somewhat confused look on his face.

"Ok, I haven't negotiated anything yet so let me know what you would feel comfortable with."

I told him *"I just want to see my kids."*

He went back in and 10 more minutes passed before he came back. He looked at me and said *"They said that they are scared. I tried setting up a meeting with police escort but they turned it down..."* Looking puzzled he asked me *"Who the hell are you?"*

I explained to him that I was just a simple man who loves his kids. All the games that they were playing are now catching up with them and that's where the fear was coming from. My lawyer said that at that point there was nothing that he or I could do. The protective order was dropped and my case in Georgia was soon to be on the way.

"Just tough it out a little while longer until your case is heard in Georgia. You don't want to do anything stupid right now, because you know if you go to see them then anything can happen." He was right, anything could happen. So we shook on it and I gave him my word that I would not pursue them and just leave it alone. I'd go back to Georgia and wait on the trial date.

Now that the protective order was lifted I just wanted to reach out to my daughter to see how she was doing. I knew what school she went to, so I called. I used to do service work for the school so I knew the maintenance staff pretty well and knew the principal as well. I pulled up the school's number on my phone and called. I spoke to the principal and faxed over a copy of the order, showing that it was lifted. I also asked speak with her and my daughter's teacher, just to see how she was doing. They decided to set up a meeting.

While at the school the principal made me aware of my daughter's absence from school. In fact she hadn't been to school in the past two weeks and she was just as concerned about her well being as I was. We ended the meeting, and she wished me luck with getting in contact with Karen and being able to see my kids. I left the school and began my journey back home to Georgia. This part of my travels I hated the most—feeling despair in my heart, being tired, physically exhausted and driving 10 hours straight, was hell.

Potholes

The beginning of the trip was fine. I was driving into the evening and was planning to get back home the next morning. On the long stretch of road my mind raced between the safety of my kids and the outcome of the trial in Georgia. I already have been blessed with a victory in Maryland, but all I kept thinking about was how crazy it was and how was all of this going to play out.

I was already tired physically and emotionally, so I tried everything to stay up. I drank energy drinks, ate candy, but nothing seemed to work. I kept falling asleep while I was heading down the highway and a couple of times I awoke and found myself heading directly into a truck, a big eighteen wheeler!

When it happened the third time, I decided to get some rest at a truck stop. I was pressed to get back home so I could get back to work that next morning because I had taken enough time off. I stopped and parked and fell right to sleep.

I don't even remember how I got to the rest stop, but I was so exhausted I was simply thankful that I made it! I set my alarm for 30 minutes.

When the alarm went off, I jumped out of my sleep, yelling. I hit the brake pedal while holding on to the steering wheel. For that split second I thought that I was back on the road and had fallen asleep at the wheel again. Just then, a lady tapped on my window and asked me if I alright. I got out of the car and just laid on the cold concrete holding on to the ground as my heart raced!

I've never experienced a heart attack, but I imagined this is what it must have felt like. My whole chest was tight and my arms were numb. I was stressed. I hadn't slept for days now and my every thought were about this case and my kids well being. I lay on that wet cold concrete ground until my alarm on my phone woke me up, and then I continued my journey back to Georgia.

Once back home and back to work, I concentrated on the next step, and that was going to court in Georgia for the legitimation case, which had now turned into an all out custody battle. I spoke to my lawyer the next day and we went over the case in Maryland and how this was gonna give me a better chance at least securing joint custody of my kids.

My lawyer, always the optimist, told me that there was still a chance that she would retain custody of the kids and that I would get joint custody, even under the circumstances. Unfair, but true. Most times in court for a woman to lose any or all of her rights to her kids she has to be strung out on drugs. During this whole process that was the most popular question "Is she on drugs?" Regardless, it was still an uphill battle.

I finished my conversation with my Georgia lawyer; I went back into my office and pulled up the Maryland State website again, just to check and see how they coded my case—if it was closed or still active, I could never be too sure. I pulled up the case and alongside that one was a new one. I pulled it up and again and saw I was being charged with another case of domestic violence!

I immediately called my Maryland lawyer and told him to look it up and let me know what this one was all about.

Man! How in the world could this be happening again! I was curious; I wanted to know what the stature on this type of case was so I pulled up some information on domestic violence cases in the state of Maryland and was surprised at what I found. There was no limit on how many times a person could draw up a domestic violence case against a person.

Come on! Four days after the case was thrown out of court and I'm in another state! Since there was no statute on this type of case, it could be used as a tool of harassment. The law stated that the petitioner had to prove "without a reasonable doubt" that the respondent committed an act of violence, so it gave the petitioner; in this case her, a free ticket to just have at it with these bogus charges.

I got to it! I started writing anybody and everybody that had anything to do with government or courts in the state of Maryland. I stated that the DV law was being used as a form of harassment. I even wrote the judges that presided over the previous cases about and advised them to flag this case as harassment. I received a copy of the affidavit and it stated that I called her and threatened to do something to her. Wow and they will bring you to court over hearsay!?

I had not called her after the court date had ended and I was free of any of the made up charges she brought against me in Maryland. So I was back on the road again to answer to more lies. I appeared in court again on April 11th and the judge ordered a continuance because she did not show up to court. I argued to the judge to throw it out, because this is another lie! But they went ahead and continued the case anyway. Now I was even more convinced that the court system did not care about this. Even though it was a familiar case to them they still wanted to hear it out--unbelievable!

So I made yet one more trip and this time they finally threw it out when she did not show up again. I received a letter from the judge stating that he received my letters and that they would flag the case, just in case it came up again.

Finally! Someone listened for once. Now everything was set in Georgia, my court date was in May and it could not come quick enough! The waiting game started, and every day was my countdown. I could not concentrate on anything but the case and my kids. I had been through a lot—losing my aunt, having to deal with this clown staring me down and getting on the stand against me. Now I had put everything into perspective with the court proceedings and what they were trying to accomplish. But it was just the principal of it all. You don't snitch and don't testify, furthermore against someone you don't know! This was burning me up inside.

I was battling with right and wrong and what made sense to me. I would say that this was the time in my life that I became a man. I was already a man just by my age alone and my responsibilities, I handled my own. But in a street sense of thinking, I grew up with the "go hard" mentality. Going hard meant not letting anyone disrespect you in any way shape or form, and it would be settled by any means necessary if it came to that.

I had never accepted any form of disrespect and the idea of "I would get you back one way or another," it just did not fit right with me to be carried. I took a step back during this whole process, well, three ring circus, which was going on and really thought about my actions. I also thought about what I had to lose if I fell into this trap that they were trying to set for me.

I give all the praises to God. First, how in the world did I find out about this case? I was divinely guided; I feel there was no other way. What I was facing during that moment in time was so great that I had to summon strength in me that I did not know that I had or was capable of having. I had to think logically and also control my emotions. I wanted to strike out when I was pushed, but I stayed calm and did the opposite. All the talking and planning that they did against me wound up turning around on them and without me being on the offensive and physically trying to get back at them. I grew up mentally and was able to see what a lot of folks kept telling me, about seeing God go to work for you. So I continued on with "going hard" and with a one track mind to get this whole thing handled right.

Now the ball was in my court and my court date was approaching, but they were not done. I was at home and I get a call from a number I don't recognize. I wasn't going to answer it, but I saw it was a Maryland number. A few seconds later the same number called back and this time I picked up.

"*Hello?*"

"*James?*"

Man! It was Karen's boyfriend. What the hell does he want?!

"*Look I don't have anything to do with what y'all going through.*" I'm thinking, yeah you do. Do you have amnesia? That was you on the stand in court testifying against me right? You have a lot to do with this so what you talking about dude? You're not off the hook by a long shot! What you saying?

He gives me this line about Karen telling him that I had planned to take out his parents--yeah uh huh, kill his parents!

"*Mane, why it got to come to this, they are church going folks and they don't have anything to do with this mane, why you gonna do that huh?*"

Wow! Really? I'm supposed to have told Karen that I was going to kill your parents? He kept talking and pleading with me and at that point I just kind of zoned out and really was not listening to him until he made this comment.

"*I mean nobody tryna go to your Mom's house and do anything to her*"

What!!!! Man I lost it right there!

For one, what the hell is up with this dude? Man, he just lucky that that bamma ass shit that they pulled they lucky ewwwuuu!!! Now this!?

After I came to, I told him "*look dude listening to her is gonna get you hurt nobody thinking about your parents or even you, but now you playing with fire.*"

"*I fucks with her hard*" and I'm like well now you just about to get fucked up!

"*Look dude mind your own business, and you a dumb ass listening to her and if it means that much to you then you'll see I ain't got nothing for you; this is all about my kids! My suggestion to you is leave while you got a chance and leave me the fuck alone!*"

Wow, I could not believe it, they were really trying my patience, but there was nothing that they could do to get me off track. Too late! The week of the court date, my lawyer calls me and tells me that it is being pushed back to a later date. I was so anxious to get this thing over with and now I have to wait out another couple of weeks. The judge presiding over our case had cancer and had gotten sick. Yes, I was upset but I looked at it this way: It was all in God's hands now so I would accept whatever happened from this point on.

Change Gon' Come

Finally, the day was here!

I had taken off from work and got up early in the morning to get ready. Today was the day that I would have my chance in court and get all of this done, so I could make it official and now have my rights. No more of her playing games with the kids and courts.

I said a prayer on the way out of the house that morning. *"God thank you for looking out for me this long and keep continuing to look out for my kids and, keep them healthy and strong. Please make a way that I will be able to be in their lives and go out and touch the hearts of the judge and my lawyer to see that I am worthy and a good man who cares for his kids, that they will make the right decision and that you will touch the hearts of those who want to see me suffer and turn them to you and grant me favor today. You know my heart and I want to do the best for my kids and be there for them. God give me more strength today, guide my mind and my tongue, so I can say and think the best things. Amen"*

I drove to the courthouse; I called my lawyer and my friend on the way to let them know that I would meet them there. As usual I arrived early, and I scanned the parking lot to see if I recognized any cars there just seeing if she had made it there also. Once I settled down in my seat they hadn't started roll call yet so I got to speak with my lawyer. He informed me that Karen had called the judge earlier that morning and had faxed in an affidavit of employment and earnings. Apparently, she still thought that I would have to pay more child support to her if she penciled in a higher rate of pay on my half of the document. I kept looking around as the courtroom began to fill up and I did not see any signs of her.

As I sat in court I thought about everything that had happened to get me here, I reflected on how much I learned about myself and the legal process and all the steps it took. It felt like my interest and determination was finally paying off. I felt a feeling of accomplishment. I took a deep breath and smiled to myself. I was proud of me and relieved that it was almost over.

Taking a look around the court room, I wondered, as I looked at the people seated, what was their road like and how did they get here. There was one case where this guy who was already in jail for domestic violence against his baby momma and other charges. He was defending himself. He had his baby momma and his current girlfriend there.

The crazy part about this was that this time he was actually taking his baby momma to court! He was locked up but was able to bring a court case against her for her throwing away his clothes and defamation of character; she accused him of being a "male whore." This was one of the wildest cases that I ever seen in my life—one for the books I tell you.

In his own defense the guy kept bumping heads with the judge. He said that he has been studying in the law library and knew what he was talking about. The judge had to shut him down. He had no chance, but that did not stop him from trying. He just thought that just because he was studying the law in the law library all of a sudden he was a lawyer. He started arguing his point and told the judge "No you're wrong." She promptly directed the deputy to send him back to jail. My man was at least trying,

The judge got to our case on the roll call and at that time I did not see Karen, but the judge added "I received a call from Karen earlier this morning at 8am. She stated that she was having car trouble and that she was in Macon. The scheduled court time was 8:30, but the judge said that she would proceed with the other cases and give her time to show up to court.

"I will give her until 11:30 to show up."

So once again we waited and watched the other cases unfold. Almost two and a half hours went by and still no sign of Karen. The judge called our case again; she went over again that she had received one call from Karen and that she was not present, "no call no show." She advised us to state our case.

Now what had begun as a case for

legitimation and child support had turned into a full out custody case. I had made up my mind after all of the drama from Maryland that I wanted to press the issue on custody. I kept telling myself that I would get custody or at least joint custody, but really having a hard time believing myself because of how the system catered to mothers first. My situation however was different.

My lawyer, in response to the judge's account of Karen's phone call and statement, told the judge *"I would not believe anything that woman says...wouldn't believe her if she said the sky was blue?"* He added *"Your Honor, I have never had a client who was so into getting his case heard; the only difference between me and Mr. Simms is that I have a 5 year degree...as you would know best about his determination."*

"Yes I have the letters to prove it," said the judge.

During this whole process I went at it full steam ahead and researched all that I needed to know and all the while sent letters to the judge to explain my situation and to keep me in the front of their minds. I figured that I needed all the proof that I could present in order to come out with the best results for the kid's sake.

The judge addressed me, *"since she is not here, we will now begin without her, so what say you."*

I began with my dedication to my family and to my kids... "Your Honor, I have always been there for my kids since their birth and even raised a child that was not my own. I am here to show my commitment to them and wanting the best for them..."

I spoke about my relationship with my kid's mother and how it all ended and also about the Maryland courts case and the outcome of that case. After I was done, the judge made her decision, *"well what I have here is a financial affidavit that shows her income that she faxed over to me this morning, let me calculate this."*

After she made her calculations she said, *"it is the judgment of the court that you Mr. Simms are granted full custody of your kids and I also order child support to be paid by the non custodial parent."*

My heart dropped!

What?

I was stunned! I never ever thought that this could ever happen. Me. Getting full custody of my kids! I did not see that coming. I had assumed that it would be joint custody and that I would receive rights to see my kids and that's it. I asked the judge to repeat that again, and she said you get full custody of the kids.

"So how will I get them back then?'

She said that it was not up to her and that I would have to petition a Maryland court for that to be handled, so I still had a ways to go.

I felt a weight lifted off of my shoulders but still left with uncertainty. How would I get them back? My first thought was to just go back to Maryland with the papers and bum rush and get my kids. At the look of it, my lawyer was shocked also. We faced each other and shook hands, and I looked at my friend and she shook her head and smiled. She had been there from day one and knew firsthand what I was going through.

The judge dismissed us and we went to a meeting room to discuss the outcome and finish up some paperwork. While we were in the meeting room my phone rings and it's Karen. My lawyer told me to play it off. *"Don't let her know anything,"* he said.

So I answered the phone, *"Hello ...Hello so what happened?"* Karen asked.

"How come you did not show up, I have to take off from work again? I can't keep doing this." I said.

Then Karen started in *"Aww you didn't get what you want, ha-ha haa!!"* and by that time I just tuned her out and let my friend and lawyer hear for themselves. I hung up the phone and my lawyer went back into the courtroom to talk to the judge. *"Unbelievable. Well, not really,"* my lawyer said. *"I wish you luck on getting them back and now you would have to go to Maryland and get this order enrolled..."* I had success at last but still a long road ahead of me, but I was prepared for the next step... getting my kids back.

Road Warrior

So I was back on the road again, and this time I had legal documentation that I had rights, sole rights to my kids. I took off two days from work so that I could drive up to Maryland and enroll the Georgia custody into Maryland.

First, I had no clue of which department handled enrolling my custody papers. I spent 2 hours in line at the main courthouse just to hear that I was in the wrong place. The clerk told me that I needed to go over to another building. I walked over and waited another hour and a half and paid $105 to have my custody papers enrolled into the Maryland system. I also had to file an emergency hearing, which I thought was going to help my situation out in getting my kids back. I had gotten wrong information, which I would find out later which would be a waste of money and time.

Eventually, I was directed to go back over to the main courthouse and wait to see a judge. I wanted for about 4 hours. While waiting, I started to build my case again. The results from my testimony could make or break this case so I wanted to be on point and have all of my ducks in a row. Finally, I was called to go in front of the judge. I remember there were only me and another person in the courtroom and this lady was trying to get an emergency hearing to get her boyfriend locked up for violating a stay away order. It didn't seem like the judge even cared about this woman's issues. He kept asking her "well did he get served with the proper paperwork," and I'm like damn, it should be cut and dry. He violated the order, file it and go lock him up! Simple! But it seemed like she did not get what she came there for and left the courtroom crying.

Now it was my turn to speak my peace and discuss my issues and the judge did not seem that receptive to my matter. He read what I wrote on the sheet of paper that I had to fill out when I registered my custody papers in Maryland. He looked over my custody papers and said "*It's not that I don't believe you, but I would like to hear her side*"

What!? Her side? Dude, she had her chance to say her side back in Georgia! He stated that this was an Emergency Hearing and that both parties had to be present, but that's not what I was told when I was filling out the paperwork. I thought that the whole purpose of doing the emergency hearing was for them to push the custody papers through quicker and for them to help in locating my kids. I wasted 6 hours plus and $105. At this point, I'm sure I was not gonna find her to serve her with this paperwork. Man you got to be kidding me! I came all the way out here and this is what I get.

I must have been too tired to think because

I normally would have researched and thought it through before making that move. I was just so anxious to get this thing done and over with and get my kids. I left the courthouse and just sat in my car and took time to think. I decided to just call the local police and check with the Marshal's office maybe then I could get something done. I called the Marshal's office and was able to get an officer to come out and meet me. I started with her sister's house. I took my custody paperwork over to the local police department in the area. They agreed to meet me at each location just in case she was there. I came up with nothing; she was nowhere to be found so I just left a copy of the certified custody paperwork at her family member's homes. I also called and talked to Karen's baby daddy to see if he had heard from her or not. Once again, I came up empty handed, the court did not recognize my order from Georgia and I could not find her or the kids so I headed back to Georgia.

The morning I arrived in Georgia I was feeling the weight of the long ride and the stress of all that I was going through emotionally, I just wanted to get in the house and go to sleep. As I was settling down in the bed my phone went off and it was Karen.

"*I see that you won full custody of the kids.*"

"*Yeah, where are you?*" I asked.
She did not respond to my question. So I

told her to call my dad and meet with him to take the kids to him, I had just drove 12 hours straight, and he could bring them down here to me. She was upset and started yelling *"No I'm not going to do that, not getting your dad into this!"*

So when I asked her when she was going to do it she hung up. I was so tired I just went to bed and when I woke I made a couple of calls. I needed help in getting my kids back. I called the night watch commander with the FBI to see what other options we had and faxed him a copy of the court order. I also called some other friends to help out and get an eye on them I had to take it to the streets. I even called in a favor from one of my close friends and gave them the rundown of what was going on and what to do when they saw my kids. I needed to keep an eye on them because it seemed like Maryland was not going to enforce my Georgia decision, but the FBI recognized the order so I had to have them spotted first and relay the info to them to where to go and pick them up. So I stayed patient.

About two weeks had gone by when I received another phone call and this was the boyfriend again and this time he had a new threat to make. He started off telling me to stop what I was doing because it is stressing Karen out. Wow, the nerve of this dude to call and tell me what to do! By this time it had become comical to me because now there was nothing in the world that any of them could do to change anything and now

I was more annoyed then what I was before. He said that she was so stressed out that she was talking about committing suicide.

Right then and there everything changed. No more patience and now it was time to act. I went to court the next day and filed for a warrant. This was gonna now get the FBI on the ground once I had her located.

I kept in contact with my folks, I had enough so now I had to call the dogs, and give them specific instructions. With everything going on I had to stay focused and could not let my emotions or even my friends emotions get us in trouble, so I asked them to just follow them and when they had eyes on them not do anything, just report back to me. I went in front of the judge for the warrant hearing and told them my concerns and give them a copy of the custody paperwork. They approved the warrant and set a court date.

I went to my lawyer's office and talked to him and we went over all of the possibilities and how I should prepare for what's coming up and he wished me luck. A couple of weeks passed and the warrant trial was quickly approaching, I had gotten word from my folks that they had spotted Karen and the kids and that they were no longer in Maryland, they were heading south. They'd gone to South Carolina to the beach and then on to North Carolina for a while. And like clockwork I had received another call from Karen's boyfriend, again trying to express to me how he felt about the whole situation, but by that time I had the jump on him. I found out everything about this dude, where he worked, lived and even hung out.

Right after that conversation had ended I got a call from Karen's cousin, I guess she wanted to add her two cents in. Apparently, during my travels to Maryland, they had heard about me looking for her and my discussions with her boyfriend and the rumor was still that I was gonna take the boyfriend's family out. He hung around an area where I had family and friends and they wanted so bad to put their hands on him but I called them off. My thing was that one day he would have to answer to all this bullshit that he and she were staring up. Her cousin started questioning me about something that was supposedly said to another one of her family members when I visited their home to drop off a copy of the custody papers. The rumor was that I was going to find his family and take them out and now they were in my ear with this nonsense again. I hung up on her and called my folks and let them know that it was about to get real thick and I wanted them to make a move as soon as they could. My plan was to get it into this dudes mind that I'm not playing anymore. I made it known to them that I knew where they were and it did not matter where they ran to but they were gonna get caught and I made a suggestion to just turn yourself in, it was over!

Judgment Day

The morning of June 11, 2008, I woke up and first thing I did was fall to my knees and thank God for his grace and his blessings. I knew that my faith in Him brought me this far and kept me from doing something that I could not reverse. I reflected on my journey and prepared myself for the day.

I called my mother and took some spiritual direction. She told me that I needed to conduct myself while I was in court because everything could get turned around. She said *"watch your attitude, don't react to anything that Karen has to say, cooler heads will prevail."*

I assured her that I was prepared and would heed to her wisdom and follow it to the T. I had worked on this case for so long, that it had become second nature and that I had all the evidence to present a good case if need be. The facts would speak for themselves.

I kept in mind that things could change, even though I had been awarded full custody of my kids it still was not over. The judge could actually overturn the judgment set by the original judge so I had to be on point. I had called the same friend who had helped me out following Karen and the kids to keep tabs on them, because I was worried that something may happen to them. He assured me that they were in Georgia and I should see them at court.

That was good news, finally I would get to see my kids and also have the chance to address all of this drama and get done with it. I called my lawyer in Maryland and my lawyer in Georgia to let them know that I was headed to court and they both congratulated and wished me luck. Once I arrived, I sat outside the door of the courtroom and went over my case in my head –what I was gonna say and do. I had about 5 more minutes until they were going to open up the doors, so I went over to the door and read the docket, just to double check.

As I was reading I heard a voice yell out *"That's my daddy!"* as I turned around I saw Karen, her friend, boyfriend and the kids walking down the hallway.

Wow! I hadn't seen my son in a while and last time I had seen him he was not talking as much or at least to say that!

I was filled with so many emotions. I was happy to see my kids and just about to go off seeing Karen, her friend and boyfriends' faces. I had a few choice words for them, but had to keep it peaceful. I gathered myself together and went over to them as they sat down, I reached out to pick my son up and Karen snatched him back *"Not until after the court case is over,"* as she gave me a snarl.

I backed up, and stared at them all, looked over to my daughter, she was looking back up at me kind of shying away not showing her emotions, as if to say she was holding back her excitement because of her mother's reaction to me reaching out to my son.

"*Hey baby how you doing?*" I asked and she replied, "*I'm good daddy.*" I turned around and headed into the courtroom. I thought back to what my mom told me and focused on the reason that I was there, found me a seat and meditated as we waited. They all sat down together just ahead of me and the kids kept turning around looking for me. My son would not stop talking and was interrupting the court proceedings. The judge ordered the kids out of the courtroom and they left out with Karen's boyfriend.

The judge opened up the cases by first introducing herself and letting everyone know of her rules "*First and most important, I do 98 percent of the listening in my courtroom and I expect that you all do the same respect each other's turn and we should get through the proceedings.*" We sat through a couple of cases and then it was time for us to go up. The judge went through all of the introductions and she started with the opening questions. "*What is the reason for this hearing today?*" she directed the questioning to me.

"*Well your honor I was awarded full custody of my kids back on May 22 and since then their mother had not given them back.*"

Karen snarled and the judge drew her

attention to her, and then she told me to continue. I had to start from the beginning from when we broke up and the day she left with my son and step daughter and left Mya with me. As I was nearing the middle of my testimony about me calling CPS and starting an investigation Karen jumped up. *"Yeah he was trying to build a personal relationship with the lady and she had to hang up on him!"* From that point on she had the floor so I just sat down. The judge looked over at me and shrugged her shoulders.

Karen went on and on about her not having any help and that no investigation was done in the matter of the abuse case that she brought against me in Maryland. She even brought up that she had taken my daughter to a therapist and had some paperwork that she had handed to the judge as evidence of this fact. The judge directed me to speak again and once again I was interrupted by Karen, so I did not object and just sat down.

This time she took the floor for what had seemed an hour. I remember I started to tune her out and just look up at the ceiling, the AC was on full blast and it was cold sitting there. I noticed that during all the commotion the Sheriff Deputies had come over and stood between us. As she spoke I was getting my response together and all of my paperwork together, the judge was looking for a way to settle this case and all the information had to be presented to her in the right manner. The judge had already consented to knowing that I had full custody granted to me from another judge but I guess the type of ruling she was going to make was gonna be determined with what she heard from either side. Finally, the judge gave me a chance to finish my side of the story.

"Your Honor I would just like to say that I have proof to show that all that she is saying is a lie and I want to defend my character. Everything that I did was for the sake of my kids. I have shown the court that I am a fit parent and a man who cares about his kids and that's why the court made the decision to grant me full custody and I have some paperwork that will disprove her case."

I handed my paperwork into evidence and went over some key facts. If she cared about her kids why would she go through lying and making up things in another court? I had paperwork showing my character. I had letters from my daughter's doctors, teachers and babysitter and also letters from my classmates and employees to show my character. Also, I had proof that when she made the call to me that she was in Georgia at the time at her girlfriend's house at 502 Marion Way and the judge asked "and how far is that from 402 Marion Way?" it's across the court, I added.

The judge took all the paper work except the ones from my classmates and employees. She took a break and said that she would review the information and get back to us. As the judge looked over the information I just sat there and said a prayer and thanked God, my aunt, mom, and my friends for all the help. Amen.

The judge came back

"...as I said earlier that I do 98 percent of the listening and I expected you all to do the same and we did not have that happen today." She directed her attention to Karen. *"Now I have read over all of the information and it seems that Mr. Simms does indeed love his kids and was doing the right thing by standing up as a man to take care of them and wanting to be in their life, why would this come to this? I have just a couple of questions for you, why after finding out that he had custody of the kids did you not just bring them back?"*

"He was gonna do what he wanted to do" Karen responded, which did not answer the judge's question. The judge had a copy of all accounts in the paperwork and I had other information to support this in my paperwork.

"Well he said that he was going to get his street team to come after me," the judge looked my way, and I said *"I did but they did not do anything to her or her boyfriend, they were just looking out for my kids to make sure that they were ok."*

"Listen," the judge said, "I'm going to ask you a very important question now. How many times after finding out that he had custody of the kids were you in the state of Georgia, and where did you go"?

That was a loaded question by the judge, she already knew that Karen had come and gone through Georgia, but she wanted to see what she would admit to. Karen said told her a couple of times and when she left she went to North Carolina. Then added that I knew where she was and knew where her boyfriend worked.

"Why, if this is true that Mr. Simms had committed a crime, why not address it in the first place with the Georgia court system?"

She had no response and the judge bowed her head. "With this, I have made my decision and change the charge to interstate interference to custody, which is a felony and at this time I will have to reprimand you over to the deputies."

Karen stood up and the deputies escorted her into the open door. She went kicking and crying into the doorway.

Her friend had an outburst *"that motherfucka betta not comes to my door!"*

The judge called to her "who are you?"

"I'm her friend!" and with a muffled sentence that ended with *"...my mother!"*

The judge interrupted her and said *"if I hear from Mr. Simms that you or your mother is harassing him, I will put you and your mother in jail. Is that clear?"*

She hurried up out of the courtroom as she nodded to the judge. The judge had made her ruling and it was final. I was relieved. She just shook her head and looked at me.

"Be careful of how you handle this situation, with your kids. Let them know that their mom will be away for a while. Don't talk bad

about this situation. Just try and move on with your lives and take care of your babies, they need you to be there for them."

I nodded. "*I will, and thank you, all I wanted to ever do was to be there for my kids.*"

The judge said that the case was over, handed me back my paperwork and said, "*Mr. Simms go and get your kids.*"

As I left the courtroom, a couple of people applauded for me and nodded their heads in appreciation. I was ready to get my kids and begin a new life.

I walked out of the courtroom and first person I saw was Karen's boyfriend. He jumped up and asked me what happened. I told him she'd been arrested. I was just itching to haul off and punch him dead in the face. He saw my expression and he backed up a little. Karen's girlfriend was sitting on the bench crying and uttering something I could not make out. I tuned everyone out and just stared at my kids. I was just in a state of content and anger all at once.

Karen's boyfriend said, "*We have their stuff in the car.*"

"*Don't worry. Keep it. I will buy them new things.*"

Karen's girlfriend pleaded with me, "*Please don't take her away from me. Make sure I will be able to see her please.*" she begged.

The deputies came in and ordered "*let them go.*"

I grabbed my kid's hands—my son on the left and my daughter on the right. As we started to walk away I looked back. The deputies made Karen's boyfriend and friend sit down as we walked away. I realized that everything that I had to endure was worth it. The sun was shining so bright, and suddenly I had an out of body experience. I could see us walking down that hallway, seeing me holding their hands and looking down at them. I was walking tall I looked down at my daughter

"*Hey baby I missed you.*"

"*I missed you daddy.*"

My son was smiling and giggling. He was happy. I looked into my daughter's eyes and I could see that she was tired. I told her everything was going to be alright.

We walked out of the court house and we had an audience. The guards who were familiar with seeing my face from week to week all said "*Congratulations!*"

Once we left the first place I took them to my job. I did not expect that I would actually have my kids today so it was a surprise. When we arrived, I told my boss that it was over and I had gotten my kids. He gave me the rest of the day off and congratulated me. Once back home, I asked my kids if they were hungry and in unison they said "yeah!" I made them both some food. My son tore through his and wanted more. My daughter was tired she was nodding in and out of sleep. I showed her, her new room. She was excited about it she now had a bunk bed. I had even cut their names out of poster board and colored them and put them up on the wall. I told her that she could go to bed and she was so excited.

"Daddy I'm so happy to be back and have my own bed!"

She went to sleep and my son asked me could he have some cereal so I gave him a bowl. Now he was just a skinny little dude and I could not believe my eyes that he had such an appetite. He still had some nuggets left after he crushed the cereal, and he started to choke on them as he was eating.

"Slow down buddy, it's not going anywhere" I told him.

After he was done with the nuggets he asked me for a sandwich. He finished it and sat there staring at the plate. I went to get the plate to put it in the sink and he started to grab my hand and screamed holding on to the plate and my hand. I let go of the plate, and sat down next to him!

My heart just sunk to my stomach. I could not hold it back the tears just started to run. I cried for about ten minutes holding his hand and him wiping the tears away, saying, *"Daddy it's ok."*

So many thoughts hit my mind right at that moment. I remembered the conversation that I had with my mother and how my concern was about the treatment of my kids. I called my mom and shared with her the good news and she said "well

God gave them back to you just in time."

Just hearing that Karen was about to commit suicide really had me on edge. Right around that time this guy in Maryland had killed himself and his kids because he did not want to split custody with his wife and I did not want that to be my situation. I was blessed to have my kids back with me just in time. By the time I got off the phone, my son was asleep. I sat and watched them both. They were so peaceful. I prayed over them and thanked God again.

Later that day my phone was ringing off the hook, everybody was calling me and wanting to know what was going on. Karen's mother, father and friends kept blowing my phone up wanting an explanation. One of her friends called me and told me that her bond was $20,000 and that she and her mom were planning to put up the money for her to get out and even putting up their house.

She said that she did not belong in jail and that if the tables were turned that Karen would speak up for me to get out of jail. She had no idea that, if the tables were turned, better yet if they had gotten their way, I would be in jail right now and I doubt if they would feel for me.

I can remember when Karen was determined to get me thrown in jail. I told her the fate that she wanted for me will be her own. So now we had come full circle and everyone wants to call and have some type of concern.

I even got a call from "Super Thug" himself! He reconfirmed the bond amount and told me that the only person that could get her out was the one who put her there.

I said" *I know you're not talking about me, cause the last time I checked she got her own self put in jail.*"

"*Man, it's rough. It's 20,000.*"

"*You're her man...you get her out!*"

The audacity of this dude, to call me and ask me to do anything to help him or her after all that they tried to do to me. I cut my phone off and just ignored them all together. I had no time for anymore drama. I was done and my kids deserved my undivided attention. It was time to be a full-time parent.

It was a long road for me, during which, I changed for the better. I feel that all of the things that I experienced happened for a reason and I am forever grateful for the experience. Faced with what would have seem to be an extraordinary feat, I overcame and stayed determined and focused on what meant the world to me, the wellbeing of my kids and preservation of myself.

My journey was not completed without the help of many, family and friends who helped me to redirect my anger at times and grab hold of faith instead of being reactive. I cannot leave out the chance meeting with the officer who gave me a road map on how to CYA, because that meeting really laid the ground work and opened up something inside of me that would help me in the long run, note taking! You wouldn't believe how much that helped me. In fact, it saved my life...

I would say through my experience, I grew up. I was shown that my behavior and way of thinking worked in most cases with the exception of this one. Reacting to what was going on around me, being my old self would have gotten me in a lot of trouble. I would have been in someone's jail and not publishing and writing books. So I say that I became a man. A man that can testify to the greatness of having faith, standing on your morals, standing your ground and taking your life's direction in your own hands. I encourage you to do the same!

No matter what you are facing, have faith and see it through. Make up in your mind that you want the best out of the situation and build a road map for yourself on how you will get through to the end.

Unfortunately, in my story a parent lost sight of what is most important—kids that needed and still need two loving parents.

Remember, that even if you cannot get along, that you need to at least be able to look past your differences and be parents for your children. My story shines a spotlight on a very serious problem that needs to be addressed. So many of us are having kids out of wedlock, single mothers, deadbeat dads and moms, and child support hell. My hope is that whoever has read this book can see either themselves, or someone they know within these pages and, worst case scenario—use it to try to learn from my story.

For those who do not have kids yet, take from my story and learn that you need to think things through before entering a relationship. Think first.

About the Author

James R Simms is from the Washington D.C area. He spent his childhood years in Arlington, VA. He grew up on the south side of Arlington in the Nauck Community, affectionately known as "Green Valley." An '80's baby, exposed to the drug epidemic and being raised by a single mother of three, his early life experiences shaped and molded his mind, and in part had a major influence on who he has become today. James attributes his background and upbringing to his ability to adapt and make something out of nothing—being poor and determined to use all his skill sets learned from the school house and the streets. Not much of a follower, he did things on his own, and lived his life by his own motto "I do my dirt all by my lonely." By all accounts, he stayed under the radar, staying grounded in the morals his mother and grandmother instilled in him, "do well in school, listen and learn…because that's one thing that no one can take from you, what you have up here," (as they would gesture with their fingers to their heads). He stayed studious and active in sports through school and into college. Temptation and old ills in life brought him back to a place that he was all too familiar with, the drug culture and financial demands. He battled with the flesh and his morality. He was never too far away from his moral base, and was able to break away and rededicate himself to living out his dreams and being the man his family had known him to be. He is now a single father of two, living in the Atlanta, GA area, currently working on more books and other projects for the near future.